I0732059

# Hunting Camp

## When hunters become the hunted

# Gin Matters

Copyright © 2021 by Hot Tub Writing, LLC

All rights reserved. No part of this book may be reproduced or transmitted in any form by any means, electronic or mechanical, including photocopying and recording, or by any information storage or retrieval system, except as may be expressly permitted by the
1976 Copyright Act or in writing from the publisher.

Rights and Permissions: hottubwritingllc@gmail.com

This is a work of fiction. Names, characters, places, and incidents either are the product of the author's imagination or are used fictitiously. Any resemblance to actual persons, living or dead, events, or locales is entirely coincidental.



Cover Artist: Shawn Rohe
Designer: Jeanna Wiggins

Paperback ISBN: 978-1-7370936-1-9
E-book ISBN: 978-1-7370936-0-2

LCCN: 2021909035

Hot Tub Writing
Bloomingdale, New York

First Edition

Printed in the United States of America

# Contents

# CHAPTER ONE

# The Biogen Farm

The Weller Group opened up a biomedical engineering facility in the heart of the Adirondack Mountains on a remote piece of land in Ray Brook, sandwiched between the villages of Saranac Lake and Lake Placid. It was a great location for a research laboratory, isolated by the surrounding lakes and mountains. The surrounding villages supported a population of just over twenty thousand people. The Adirondack Park Forest Preserve was established in the 1890's. The locals referred to it as, "The Blue Line"—over six million acres, including several undersized hamlets, designated as a National Historic Landmark in 1963. It was a perfect place to experiment and create.

The local municipalities were happy to have an outside business enter the area and infuse money into the local economies. So, they didn't ask questions like, "What exactly are you doing in your facility?" In fact, another long-term research center had already been established there: the Trudeau Institute, which helped battle tuberculosis in the 19th and 20th centuries. Since then it transitioned to researching other diseases and became renowned worldwide. The Weller Group easily hid their secret research laboratory in Trudeau's shadow.

Troy Parker had been employed by Weller Group for the past three years. He was hired as a utility specialist. The title, "utility specialist", was an umbrella that encompassed several jobs. Security, buildings and grounds, general maintenance and today, delivery man. He drove a box of lab samples to the Lake Clear Airport about seven miles out of town. His colleague, Joey, rode shotgun. It was a simple request from Dr. Yogerra: drive the samples to the airport and rendezvous with the transporter, where the samples would be placed on the company jet.

It was a wet December day. The road was slushy from last night's snow. They had just passed Donnelley's Corner and were a few miles away from the airport.

"Leave it alone!" Joey said looking over at Troy.

Troy shook his head. "This song sucks!"

"I like it."

Suddenly the van swerved. The wheels vibrated loudly as the vehicle crossed over the yellow line.

"Just keep your eyes on the road!" Joey said.

Troy surveyed the road but saw nothing. He then looked back down to the stereo. Keeping his left hand on the wheel, he reached for and pressed the tuning button.

"Deer!"

Troy immediately looked up, but it was too late. He saw the buck running in from the left, then the van hit it. The collision was a strange combination of thumping and crunching sounds. The noise resonated deep down into Troy's soul. The deer disappeared over the vehicle. Instinctively, he pulled the vehicle hard to the right. The tires squealed and the van flipped over, rolling several times before sliding to a halt off the right side of the road.

Time seemed to have slowed. Troy was disoriented. His stomach was queasy, and his vision was a little blurry. He could still hear the engine running. He wiggled his toes and then his fingers. Troy started twisting his body and moving his arms and legs. He seemed all right. He noticed his airbag had not deployed. He then turned his head and noticed Joey's bag hadn't either.

"Are you ok?"

Joey nodded. Troy suddenly became aware of uncomfortable pressure in his lower abdomen from his seatbelt. They were upside down. He was currently sporting long hair and it flowed down towards his shoulders. Now, it was hanging in his face.

Troy reached over and turned the engine off. He unstrapped his seat belt and opened the door. He had to roll to his left side and shimmy outside. Troy noticed Joey exiting the passenger side. Before he got to his feet, he could hear Joey throwing up. Troy surveyed the scene, the buck lay on its side, motionless. Troy moved closer.

"Hey, Joey, come help me." Joey coughed "Give me a minute, I'm dying over here!"

Troy glared back at Joey.

"Someone else is going to die if we don't get this thing out of the road!"

Joey pushed himself up and stumbled over to where Troy was. For a moment they just stood over it, looking. It looked like it had passed on. There didn't seem to be any physical damage to its extremities but there was blood dripping from its mouth.

"Is it dead?" Joey asked Troy.

"Looks dead!"

They grabbed it by the legs and dragged it to the van. Joey started complaining about his right arm. A few moments later another car stopped. The driver asked if we were ok. He then used his cell phone and called in the accident. Then a little while after that, the State Troopers showed up. They started questioning Joey and me. Asked if we had been drinking alcohol. They were concerned about Joey's injuries, so they radioed into their headquarters for an ambulance. Within thirty minutes it was like a carnival, complete with an ambulance, tow truck and two more state trooper vehicles. After the paramedics determined he was fine, Troy called Dr. Yogerra. She was our boss. She ran the Biogen research facility in Ray brook. There was nothing pleasant about her. Troy didn't like her, nobody liked her. She was all business. After he hung up the phone, Troy wondered if he still had a job. She was not happy. She didn't care that Joey had to go to the hospital. All she cared about was the samples. Troy had to guard the samples until another company van could arrive and take responsibility for them. As he walked away from the ambulance, he noticed that the back door of the van was open. A state trooper was looking inside.

"Excuse me, sir, can I help you?"

The trooper turned around and looked at Troy. He seemed annoyed. An uncomfortable silence lasted between the two of them for several seconds.

"What is this stuff? In the box?"

Troy noticed that the box was leaking. It was leaking all over the dead deer. It had a green radio-active color that seemed to be surrounded by a red mist. It smelled like strong battery acid.

"I don't know. I'm just the driver!" To Troy, it seemed like he was being interrogated. Like he was transporting illegal contraband.

The trooper examined the deer. He took a long time studying it.

"Hey, you gonna keep the deer?"

Troy didn't understand the question at first. He wasn't from the Adirondacks. He grew up in Nevada. He transferred up when the company opened the new facility. Troy hated the cold, and he wasn't crazy about eating venison, but the locals were nuts about it. They hunted and ate these poor bastards all the time. It made no sense to Troy. Why not just go to the store and buy a steak?

"No," he said. "You can have it."

The trooper smiled and grabbed his radio.

"Hey Travis, you have your ears on over?"

"Copy that, over!"

"We have a roadkill out here on 30, about two miles from the airport. It's a buck, six pointer. Probably hundred twenty lbs. Over."

The trooper turned away from Troy and started walking towards his vehicle. Troy noticed how bright the flashing lights were from the patrol car. Troy hated those lights, they always made him feel like he was doing something wrong. He then walked over and said goodbye to Joey before the ambulance pulled away. The paramedics said he had a concussion and a possible broken arm.

The company van pulled up about ten minutes later. George was driving.

"You doing ok?" He asked.

Troy nodded.

To his surprise, he noticed Dr. Yogerra emerged from the van. She walked right past him, her eyes on the box of samples. She stopped, turned and gave Troy a piercing look.

"The samples have been compromised."

She spoke with a thick European accent. She was not a tall woman, maybe five foot at best. But her stature was rigid and intimidating. Dr. Yogerra had black straight hair about shoulder length. She wore cat eyed glasses and always fashioned the same black pant suit. Her hands were covered with Thermo Scientific Waterproof Cryo Gloves. A very expensive specialized glove that was designed to operate in very cold temperatures. Troy had used these gloves before working with Dr. Yogerra in her laboratory.

George came up behind us and placed a bigger box on the ground. He opened it, and dry ice smoke rose into the air. Dr. Yogerra carefully picked up the damaged box from the van, placed it in the bigger box, and closed the lid.

George took the box back to the van and returned with a small kind of propane tank with a hose and nozzle.

Dr. Yogerra looked at him.

"Light it up. Don't get too close to the van."

George twisted the nozzle and pressed a button, converting the contraption into a flamethrower.

"Stand back!"

Dr. Yogerra didn't move, but Troy did. George torched the ground where the damaged box had been dripping, spraying the flames back and forth several times. The heat was intense, Troy could feel it hit his face. He stepped back another two steps.

"What's going on?"

A trooper ran toward the inferno, waving his hands frantically.

"Put it out! Turn it off!"

Dr. Yogerra ignored him and said to George.

"Let's go."

George turned the nozzle, and the flames disappeared. The three of them started walking back toward the other van. Dr. Yogerra turned her head and spoke to Troy.

"Don't sit on the samples in the van."

"Hey."

We stopped and turned around.

It was the trooper.

"Where's the buck?"

Troy hadn't even noticed that it was gone. His attention had been on George's miniature flamethrower.

"What is he talking about?" Dr. Yogerra said, looking at Troy.

"We hit a deer. I told you that. That's why we crashed."

Dr. Yogerra walked over to the trooper and stood behind the van studying the scorched earth. She ignored the trooper and looked up at Troy.

"Did the sample get on the deer?"

The trooper turned on Dr. Yogerra. "Just exactly what is this 'the sample'? What was in the box?

She looked at him.

"Company secrets. None of your business."

The trooper seemed more emboldened by her response.

"Lady, I can make it my business."

Dr. Yogerra pulled out her cell phone and dialed a number.

"Major Viera? Yes, this is Dr. Yogerra from the BioGen farm."

The trooper got a solemn look on his face. Major Viera was the acting state police commander at Troop B headquarters in Ray brook.

"Yes, that's right. I had a company van hit a deer. One of your troopers is on the scene right now. Would you like to talk to him? Yes, I will put him on speaker."

Dr. Yogerra smiled at the trooper. The voice on the other end said,"Who am I speaking to?"

It sounded angry.

"This is Trooper Colby, sir."

"Listen, Colby. You are to help and assist Dr. Yogerra in any way she needs. Is that clear, trooper?"

"Yes, sir, Major!"

Dr. Yogerra turned the speaker off and said goodbye to the major on the other end. She hung up and smiled at the trooper.

"Goodbye, Trooper Colby."

She didn't wait for a reply. She turned, and we all walked back to the van.

Without turning to look at him, she said, "I asked you if the sample dripped on the deer."

Troy was sure he was already on Dr. Yogerra's shit list. He didn't want to disappoint her any more than he already had. He remembered what had happened to Hector a month ago. The guy mopped up the lab floor, a daily ritual. It was part of Hector's job. Well Dr. Yogerra walked in and slipped on the wet surface. She ended up firing Hector for doing his job. Troy turned his head and was getting ready to reply to his boss. She also turned her head and looked him in the eyes, revealing no emotion, a perfect poker face.

"No, there was nothing on the deer!"

Her expression didn't change.

As we got into the van, a truck pulled up, and another guy got out and spoke to Trooper Colby.

"Where is it?"

"I don't know," Colby said. "Must have gotten up and run off into the woods."

# CHAPTER TWO

# Big Charlie

The deer had left the security of the tree line. They were hungry. In foraging, they settled upon a lush meadow. Full of grass and white clover. There were mushrooms and an abundance of hay.

There were five does, three adults and two yearlings. The leaves had been falling for some time and the trees were almost bare. The temperature was unusually warm for this time of year. The sky was full of clouds. It was a windless, calm day. Big Charlie was hidden, watching them from the tree line. He had roamed these woods with his impressive antler rack for over twenty years. This was his harem. These were his lands.

From a distance, a buck walked out of the trees toward them. All five does lifted their heads, their tails instinctively pointed straight up. The strange buck grunted. The does looked to their alpha. Big Charlie emerged from the tree line and grunted back.

Upon seeing the alpha, the smaller buck stopped in his tracks, two-hundred feet away. Big Charlie turned sideways and lifted his head up and down. This action helped him display the full size of his antlers to his opponent. The smaller buck bowed his head, took four steps backwards, and returned to the woods.

The does went back to grazing. The bucks behaved this way before the snow came. They were used to it.

Big Charlie returned to his watchful post in the tree line. It was getting late. The sun would set soon. They needed to bed down for the night. Again, the does looked up, their tails pointed in the air. Another challenge. Big Charlie stepped out of the tree line and gazed across the meadow.

A bigger buck this time, though still smaller than him. Big Charlie walked forward a few steps, turned sideways, and raised his head up and down several times. Then he turned toward his nemesis and grunted. He had not been challenged to a physical duel in a couple of years. This one was smaller. It would surely bow and run away. To Charlie's surprise, the smaller buck walked forward and seemed to grin. Charlie had never seen another buck open its mouth that way before. Its eyes squinted as it approached. It looked at the females, who were frozen in anticipation. They had not seen anyone challenge their alpha in a long time.

The smaller buck slowly closed the distance between itself and Charlie. Charlie broke into a trot, until they were separated by a deer length. Charlie raised his head up and down several times, grunting loudly.

The smaller buck stood silent. He stared at Charlie's magnificent rack. It was impressive.

There was something different about this buck. Its legs were thicker than they should be, as were its torso and neck. The eyes were different, too. They were too close, almost centered on the face.

Big Charlie had enough. He reared up on his back legs and sprang forward.

The smaller buck did the same. The collision was thunderous. With their antlers locked, the two combatants pushed and twisted. Big Charlie shoved his challenger back several deer lengths. They separated and then attacked each other again, but this time with more ferocity. Again, the noise was ear splitting. Charlie was getting stronger with each attack. Big Charlie's strength overwhelmed the smaller buck, consistently pushing it back. They collided a fourth time. The two bucks locked antlers, but this time, neither gave ground. The smaller buck suddenly seemed stronger, heavier. The smaller buck reared up on its hind legs, their locked antlers forcing Charlie to do the same. The does watched with curious fascination.

The two bucks stood that way for several seconds. The smaller buck lifted up its right hoof.

To Charlie, it looked like a claw. Charlie also noticed the claw had a bigger, sharper toe, in the middle.

It tore open Charlie's abdomen with a vertical slice. The bucks separated. The does watched as the entrails of their alpha male spilled to the ground.

The smaller buck grinned, opening its jaws to display a mouth full of raptorial teeth. Charlie fell over on his side and died.

The smaller buck walked over to the dead deer and tore at its flesh. The does watched, calmly accepting the change. They had a new alpha male.

Five months later their herd would produce seven new fawns—different fawns.

Three years later, the new herd would become the dominant species in the Adirondack mountains—the top of the food chain.

# CHAPTER THREE

## The Race

Billy screamed from the back seat, "Step on it, John!"

"Don't let those fuckers beat us to Exit 30!"

They were north of Albany on I-87 headed toward Adirondack Park. Exit 30 was where they would get off the interstate and catch route 9N. Then a-hunting, there they would go. They had just passed Exit 9, and the speed limit had just gone from 55 to 65. John could see Dan's truck up ahead, two cars away.

*Crack, pop.*

"You go Johnnie! We're gaining on those bastards," shouted Darrel from the front seat while striving to lap up the beer spilling from his Coors Light.

They were racing to the Lake Placid Horse Show grounds, about two miles outside Lake Placid proper, where the opening ceremonies for the 1980 Winter Olympics had been held. The first to get past the Olympic torch outside of Lake Placid would win. Losers had to buy dinner.

Three roads led into the Adirondack region. Route 86 came in from Plattsburgh, Route 3 was from Watertown and anyone from the capital used 9N off I-87, which connected to route 73. They would catch that in Keene. As a kid, John ate at Purdie's Elm Tree Inn, where they made the famous Purdy Burger. The Inn had pictures on the wall of what seemed like every bobsledder who ever raced. John's father had been taking them hunting in the Adirondacks since they were kids. They looked forward to the trip every year.

"They're getting away!"

John glanced at his big brother Darrel.

"You want to drive?"

Darrel was two years older. John's hair was blonde, but Darrel's was brown like their father. People called him Moose because of his size. He was an all-state linebacker in high school.

"Johnnie, you know if they get to the Cascades before us, it's over!"

Darrel was right. There were only a few spots to pass on 73. The Cascade Mountain Range was part of the Adirondack 46ers, meaning it had forty-six peaks over four thousand feet above sea level. Route 73 carved out a narrow two-lane road through the Cascades toward Lake Placid. With Cascade Lake on the left, it was impossible to pass. One slip-up and everyone in the car would have a watery grave. Hikers were everywhere too, with cars parked on the side of the road and people walking on both shoulders. It was hard to go fast on route 73.

Billy leaned forward and stuck his head between the two brothers.

"I'm going to get Big Charlie this year!"

Darrel and John smiled at each other.

"Billy, when's the last time you got a buck?" Darrel said.

With a scowl on his face, Billy delivered a quick response.

"Fuck you, Darrel!"

Big Charlie was a legend—twelve points, over twenty years old and nearly 300 pounds. Darrel had seen him once with his dad about five years before, or so they said.

"The thing is a myth!" John said. All the hunters had been talking about Big Charlie sightings for years. John assumed they were telling tall tales. Hunters were known to exaggerate how big the buck was that got away.

Darrel looked at his brother. "You know Dad wasn't a liar! We saw him that day, Johnnie."

John bristled at the childhood nickname. "It's John!"

Billy started laughing. He had grown up with Darrel and John. They all understood that John didn't like to be called Johnnie. Billy leaned a little closer to John.

"Just put the pedal to the metal Johnnie boy!"

Billy grew up two houses down the street. He was Darrel's best friend. They graduated together. They did everything together. But this last year had put a strain on Darrel and Billy's friendship. Billy was spending more time with Jill, his girlfriend. They took the next step and got an apartment together. Darrel didn't have a girlfriend. He wasn't happy that Billy was spending all his free time with Jill. Darrel was really looking forward to this trip, more so than most years. John and he had lost their father two years ago and so last year, the annual Adirondack hunting trip was put on moth balls. It didn't seem right to go without their Dad. But this year had to happen. Darrel was worried that his group was drifting away. Everyone was getting older. It was only a matter of time before someone got married or moved away. This annual trip was the glue that kept them all together.

For the next hour, they raced the other vehicle up I-87. Darrel and Billy reminisced about glory days—mostly high school football and one-night stands. John smiled and laughed. He knew most of the stories. Heck, he'd witnessed several of them. It felt good. The three of them, like old times. Maybe Billy would shoot Big Charlie. John imagined the three of them gathering around the big buck, taking a picture with Billy holding the massive twelve-point rack and everyone else raising a beer to the heavens.

"Billy boy, I need ya to get a Billy cocktail ready."

John and Billy started laughing. Darrel invented the Billy cocktail years before. On long car trips, Darrel would piss in an empty beer can. This saved time because there was no need to stop and find a bathroom. Billy downed his can of beer in two swallows. He then unzipped his fly and started urinating in his empty can. Daryl looked at his little brother. He had a devious looking grin on his face.

"Punch it when we get past Exit 25."

John nodded. They were past Exit 24 now. The state troopers thinned out farther from Albany, at least that was the general philosophy. The reality was that Darrel couldn't afford to get any more speeding tickets. He held a commercial driver license and drove an oil truck for a living. One more violation and his CDL could get suspended. This would ruin his livelihood. And Billy, he was sitting on a DWI from a year ago, said his lawyer would get it reduced to a DUI any day now. Either way, John was the NASCAR driver on this trip. Exit 25 flew by, and he kicked the engine up to eighty. We blew past a red Toyota Corolla and came up alongside our posse.

In the other truck were Dan, Sal and Karl—all the guys we grew up with and went to school with. Danny was at the wheel wearing the biggest shit-eating grin. He had just bought it a couple months before. A black Toyota Tacoma. Dan was proud of his truck. Sal and Darrel used that pride against him. They were always complaining that Dan bought a Japanese truck. That it wasn't a real truck because it wasn't made in America. Karl was already drunk before we left, and now, he looked passed out in the back seat. Sal rode shotgun. He had a dip going, which meant he had downed a six pack already. Darrel was called "Moose," but Sal was bigger than a moose. Not really, but he was a big fella: 6'4", 320lbs and gaining. Played defensive tackle in high school. He got asked to go play at Hudson Valley Community College. They were a football factory. Some guys that went there went on to play D1 college football. But they wanted him to play offensive line. He hated the offensive line. So, Sal became a truck driver like Darrel.

Darrel motioned for them to roll the window down. Karl sprang to life and scrambled for the button on the window. Billy screeched: "Fucking Karl is wasted!"

We all laughed.

Dan got his window down and glanced at Darrel for a brief second.

"What'sssss upppppp?"

Danny loved to say that.

Darrel said, "Hey, we come bearing gifts. We got

a cold one and a warm one for ya."

Travelling at eighty miles per hour, John pulled the SUV until the two vehicles were only three feet apart. Billy reached through the window and passed a cold beer to Karl, then he tossed the warm beer through the window onto Karl's lap.

"Gah! It's open asshole!"

John laughed so hard he could hardly drive. He accidentally turned the wheel to the left and this caused Darrel to spill his beer on his lap.

"What the fuck!" Darrel looked at John in disbelief.

He regained control and pulled back up to Dan.

Danny turned and shouted, "Karl what the fuck! Don't spill your beer in my truck!"

Karl looked confused. He finally turned the beer right-side up, spilling most of it over himself and the back seat in the process.

"That ain't no beer!" Karl had a look of bewilderment on his face.

Dan slowed down to look in the back seat. That's how we took the lead. We made it to Exit 30 first. From there it was a tight race through the Cascades. Forty minutes later, when we passed the Olympic torch at the horse show grounds, Billy stuck his ass out the window and screamed: "Victory Moon!"

In the rear, Danny didn't look pleased, he had a frown on his face. The kind of expression that signals defeat.

# CHAPTER FOUR

## Joey Morrow

In the village, they stopped at a mini-mart gas station. John and Danny filled up, while the others went inside to use the facilities. Karl looked like he was ready to piss his pants. He smelled like it too. So did the whole back seat of Dan's truck.

Danny called to Karl as he was walking away.

"Karl, ya better get rid of that piss smell."

This caused Billy to stop and look back at Karl. He started laughing. Karl wore a look of confusion.

"And how do ya propose I do that?"

"I'm serious. Change your clothes."

Karl went back to the truck and pilfered through his bag for a pair of jeans and a T-shirt.

"Hey," Dan shouted, "look for some white vinegar in there."

Karl gave him a drunken look.

"White vinegar?"

"Yeah, it'll get the smell out of the truck. If you can't find any, bring me some air freshener."

Karl gave Danny a thumbs up and walked toward the mini mart. As Billy opened the door for Darrel, he stopped to read a missing child poster on the door.

"Joey Morrow, age 11, 5'3", black hair, blue eyes, last seen August 23." Billy looked at Darrell with a facial expression full of disapproval.

"Even a remote place like this has kidnappings going?"

"Probably a runaway."

Billy thought about that. Maybe he was right. Maybe the kid went to live with his aunt or something.

Darrel walked into the men's room, while Billy headed to the cooler for more beer. Karl came in, heading for the bathroom. Billy made eye contact, and they both started laughing.

Karl pointed his finger at Billy and said, "Payback's a bitch, brother!"

Billy gave Karl a thumbs up then went back to browsing the beer coolers. After about a minute, he turned his attention to the counter, where Sal was buying a can of dip.

"Hey, man, do you have any Busch Light here?" Billy said.

The guy grinned as he looked away from the television that was hanging from the ceiling behind the counter.

"Oh yeah. The lattes are on the bottom to the left."

Billy looked confused. "No, I don't want coffee, I want—"

"Ya, Busch Light. Up here we call them Busch Lattes!"

Billy rolled his eyes and went back to find them. He returned to the counter with a twelve pack.

"That's not enough!" said Darrel, coming up behind him.

Billy turned around and gave his best friend an evil smile. Reluctantly, he gave up his place in line and walked back to the cooler. Darrel put a bag of chips up on the counter and looked at the clerk's name tag. "Hey, Mike?"

The clerk looked at Darrel with a confused expression. "Do I know you?"

Darrel pointed at the name tag. Mike got embarrassed.

"Hey, what do they think happened to that kid?"

Mike gave Darrel a confused look.

"The poster on the door."

"Oh, you mean little Joey Morrow."

"Yeah Joey. What happened? I thought that the Adirondacks were considered one of the safest places in New York State."

Billy had a case of Busch Lights this time. He was quick to butt into the conversation.

"Strangest thing," Mike said. "Joey's mother says

the kid went out in the woods behind his house and never came home.”

Darrel and Billy shot each other a look. Billy shrugged his shoulders and then they both turned back to Mike. Darrel asked the clerk the next question.

“Did he live outside the village?”

“Yeah, about three miles out toward Craig Wood Golf Course.”

Darrel and Billy knew where that was. They had passed it on the way into town, after the bobrun, right before the ski jumps.

Darrel looked up at the TV and then back down to Mike. “He get lost? What’s the theory floating around?”

“He was a weird kid. Loner type. Big into video games. Mom was a single parent, divorced. Some folk say his father took him—I guess he lost a custody case years ago. Others think he fell in the lake. The village is too cheap to drag the lake for the body.”

“Hey, put my chips on his beer bill. Thanks, Billy,” Darrel said, then he walked out the door toward the vehicles.

Billy shouted at his back, “Hey D-man, you owe me!”

## CHAPTER FIVE

# Hot Sara
# & the Bel

A few minutes later, they were gassed up and heading toward Saranac Lake. Ten miles after that, they checked into the famous Hotel Saranac for the night and hit up the Belvedere Restaurant for dinner. Like the race, it was tradition. One last celebration before we headed into the woods for one week to hunt. Losers buy.

John's father always had a strip steak and a side of pasta, so I always ordered that. Sometimes their father would eat off everyone else's plate. That always bothered Darrel more than it bothered John. The locals were friendly, and the place was always loud. As soon as we opened the door, the atmosphere spilled out of the restaurant and consumed us with laughter and jukebox music. The only other place their father ever talked about was the Dew Drop Inn. But that had been closed for a long time.

After dinner, everyone gathered at the bar. The winners picked up the after-dinner drinks. In honor of their father, John and Darrel started a tradition: gin martinis, straight up, three olives. This was his signature drink annually at the Bel. The bartender, Welchie, was not too keen on this tradition. The Bel wasn't a martini bar. It was more of a beer and bourbon and coke bar. Welchie could pour a draft beer, open up a bottle of beer, and on occasion, mix a bourbon and coke. Their father would have called it a gin joint. When the martinis arrived, Darrel raised his in a toast. "To Dad! Or to Butch!"

Everyone raised their martinis and saluted John and Darrel's father. Everyone choked them down except for Karl. After two sips, he became violently sick and ran to the men's room.

Something on the TV caught Sal's attention.

"Hey, check this out."

A reporter faced the camera standing next to a state trooper. He was taller than the trooper and wore a black ski jacket that sported a Channel 5 News emblem.

"This is Robert Wilson with Channel 5 News. I am talking with Lieutenant Rosen of Troop B about the ongoing investigation into the disappearance of Greg Callfield, thirty-one, from Almira New York. Lieutenant Rosen, can you tell us what happened to

Mr. Callfield? We heard that he was mauled by a pack of deer?"

The state trooper gave the camera a small smile.

"Mr. Callifield became separated from his hunting party and is presumed lost in the woods. We have no further details to report at this time."

The trooper walked away from the camera and the reporter came back into view.

"We also have a member of Mr. Callfield's hunting party. Your name, sir?"

"Burt Carpenter."

"Mr. Carpenter, what can you tell—"

"Greg was attacked by three deer."

Billy looked over at Darrel. "What the fuck did he just say?"

Burt Carpenter went on. "We were ambushed by a pack of them. Look, they bit me, here."

The TV zoomed in on the hunter's arm. It was bandaged up above the elbow, and there were blood stains oozing out from the bandage.

Danny shook his head. "Those idiots. Deer don't attack people!"

Billy nodded in agreement.

"Maybe they were rabid?" Karl said.

Darrel kept staring at the TV but said, "Rabid Deer don't hang out in packs!" The reporter continued. "It sounds like to me that a hunting party from Almira had too much to drink and now one member from their party is missing.

Everyone at the bar started laughing. Even the news reporter was laughing.

Sal started shaking his head. "Deliverance country up here, man!"

"Yeah, do they even have the internet up here?" Dan said.

They all laughed again. One guy at the end of the bar didn't though. The barkeep knew him by name, and John figured he looked like a local. Even though he was a stranger to John, he definitely wasn't a stranger to the bar. He had a quiet confidence about him, like he lived here. He was in his fifties, maybe sixty?

Darrel motioned to the bartender to outfit everyone with another drink. Beer this time! He looked down at the local at the end of the bar. "Good sir, my miscreant friends and I would like to buy you a drink."

The stranger looked at Darrel long and hard. With no expression he nodded his head and said, "I accept!"

A few minutes later everyone raised their drink and toasted for a successful future hunt. Billy added, "Big Charlie, I'm coming for you!"

Everyone started chanting, "Big Char-lie! Big Char-lie!"

After a few minutes, the chanting subsided, and

a peaceful silence rested in the bar. The jukebox was playing 38 Special's, "Hold on Loosely". Billy told the bartender to turn the music up, then he grabbed a pool stick and started lip synching.

*"Don't let go. If you cling too tightly, you're gonna lose control."*

Karl joined in with an air guitar. Sal slapped the beat on the bar with his hands. Meanwhile, John recorded the whole thing on his cell phone.

After the song was over, John and the others bellied up to the bar and ordered shots of Dr. McGillicuddy's Peppermint Schnapps—John's dad's favorite.

Darrel looked down at the end of the bar again. "Sir would you kindly join us one more time?"

The stranger again nodded his head with no expression and responded, "Yes."

We all raised our shots to heaven. Darrel spoke a toast, a poem their father always used to say: ***"Good warning to the deer, in the meadow and in the wood. Good warning to you all, to all your splendor and to all your brood. Sleep well without worry, sleep well without fear. In the morning, I will be there!"***

They downed their shots. John was impressed. Darrel had recited the poem perfectly.

Their celebration was broken by a shout from the local at the end of the bar. "Big Charlie is dead!"

The bar went completely quiet. Everyone stared

at the local for what seemed like an eternity. After a long uncomfortable silence, the barkeep gave the local a petulant look. "You don't know that, Sully. The Martin brothers were in here last Saturday saying they saw Big Charlie out by Meacham."

Darrel and the others looked at Welchie, the bartender, and then back down at the local. It got really quiet in the bar. Everyone seemed to be waiting for a response from the local. "Say friend . . . is your name Sully?"

The local nodded at Darrel.

"What happened? Who was the lucky man that brought down that majestic king!"

Sully shook his head. "Weren't no man that took Big Charlie!"

Darrel looked back at the boys and shrugged. "Coyotes?" he asked. "Did he get hit by a car?"

Billy said, "Old age! Charlie had to be in his twenties!"

"No, I bet another buck took him during the rut," said Sal.

Welchie was impatiently waiting his turn. He was nodding and pointing a finger.

"I am telling you, that he's still roaming the woods. Nobody knows these mountains better than the Martin brothers."

"And who taught them to hunt these mountains?" said Sully.

Welchie blushed. "You Sully." Welchie had known Sully his whole life. Anyone who hunted or fished in the Adirondacks knew who Sully was. Sully was a well-respected licensed guide.

Sully looked at Darrel. This time his expression was different. His eyes were dark. His face was stone cold, and his lower lip was twitching.

"Don't go in those woods!"

No one said anything. You could hear a pin drop in the silence.

Finally, Sal said, "What are you talking about, old timer?"

"It's not safe!"

Sal stood up. "We have been coming up here for the past fifteen years hunting these mountains. The only thing not safe is me shooting someone's dog with my thirty yacht six. Those fuckers are always chasing the deer away."

Darrel motioned Sal to be quiet. They all looked back over to Sully. He had their attention.

"There is something else out there in the woods."

Billy couldn't help it. "You mean Bigfoot!" he blurted.

The bar broke out in laughter. Beer sprayed out of Danny's mouth.

Welchie said, "Sully was involved in a hunting accident a couple years ago. His buddy, Pat Wheeler, was mauled by a bear."

Sully slammed his fist down on top of the bar. "Weren't no bear! A bear doesn't eviscerate a person. Pat had bite marks on him consistent with a canine."

"So, it was wolves?" asked Billy.

"There are no wolves in the Adirondacks. Maybe coyotes, or wild dogs?" Sal suggested.

Sully kept shaking his head. "I know what Pat told me before he died."

Another long uncomfortable silence as everyone waited for Sully to explain.

"He said, 'Watch out. Don't follow the big one. They are always watching. The big one sets you up. The little ones get you from the sides.'"

The only sound in the quiet that followed was the reverberation of the beer cooler behind the bar.

Darrel said, "What was he talking about, do you think?"

Sully looked out past Darrel, as if he were seeing something a thousand miles away.

"I saw the rack. Sixteen points." He focused on Darrel again. "Don't go chasing it. If you see the rack, get out of there."

Sal scowled. "There is no way a sixteen-point buck is running around the Adirondacks."

"One more thing!" Sully said. "The wind, it whispers."

Billy pointed at his head and made a gesture like the old man was crazy. Sully saw him doing it and smiled. "I've been called crazy before, but I dragged

Pat two miles out of the woods that day. He was in a lot of pain. He begged me to stop dragging him. So, I set him down about fifty yards from the road and drove to get cellular reception. The troopers arrived thirty minutes later, but when I went back to where I'd left Pat, he was gone. I started screaming for him. Pat! Pat, where are you?" The old man put his hands up to his mouth as if he were shouting.

"On the walk back to the road we could hear the wind. It was calling out to us."

Karl made eye contact with Sal, confused. "What did the wind say?"

The old timer looked at Karl. "Paaaat. Paaaaat. It kept going with the 'A' sound. Paaaaaat."

Karl was entranced. "So Pat wasn't dead?

Sully looked at him. "It wasn't Pat's voice. It didn't sound human."

Suddenly, Sully stood up from the bar, tears flowing down his face. He looked at the barkeep. "I have to go." Then he walked out the door.

Everyone sat quietly, again very uncomfortable. The sound of the reverberating beer cooler filled the room. Welchie broke the silence. "They never found Pat's body. Everyone figured Sully accidentally shot him. He served time for it. The DA tried throwing the book at him, but they could never find the body. After several months, they dropped the case. That was a year ago."

---

# CHAPTER SIX

# Forest Home Road

Cheryl was on her way home. The stars and moon were hidden by a blanket of snow clouds. Darkness lay thick on both sides of the road. Visibility would have been better if she had taken 86, but she chose her reliable shortcut, Forest Home Road. It shaved fifteen minutes off her commute. She turned on the radio. The local news was still rambling about a missing hunter from Almira. Bushy snowflakes were falling, big and beautiful, like how kids would cut them out in art class. She turned off her high beams since the snow was just reflecting the light back into her eyes. Couldn't go too fast in these conditions, especially on this road. Forest Home Road had a couple of five-mph 90-degree curves as well as a zigzag known to send many a driver off the soft shoulder into the trees. Everyone who lived outside the village in the Lake Clear area used this shortcut, especially if the driver had been drinking—troopers never patrolled Forest Home Road, staying mostly on 86.

"Greg Callfield is still missing," said the voice on the radio. "It's been twenty-four hours and authorities have not ruled out foul play."

Cheryl frowned. The radio reminded her of what happened to Mr. Wheeler. He was a close family friend. They never found his body. She was sure Sully knew more about what happened. She shook her head and reached for the dial to change the station. No dial, it was a push button stereo. She hated it, especially while you were driving. The push button was smaller and harder to find. Of course, Craig had to upgrade the stereo that came with the truck—another thousand dollars for this piece of shit! The truck itself was barely worth that. It was ten years old when they bought it last summer. She found the search button and then turned her attention back to the road. There wasn't much reception out here, and the radio soon gave up. This repeated a few more times: push the button, look up, and wait to see if the radio finds a station. Finally, the Rolling Stones belted out, *"Get off of my cloud!"*

"Success!" Cheryl proclaimed out loud when she looked up and saw a deer standing in the middle of the road. She pulled the wheel hard to the right. A line of trees loomed in front of her suddenly, so she swerved hard left again. The truck did a complete 180-degree turn and slid off the soft shoulder, coming to a stop in a low ditch off the right side of the road.

"Motherfucker!" Cheryl's heart was racing, and she was breathing fast. *Amazing what adrenaline does for you,* she thought.

The truck had stalled. She turned the key off and then back on. Nothing happened.

"Ugh, put it in park asshole!"

When she was a little girl, her mother once asked her if she was talking to herself. When Cheryl responded yes, her mother then asked her if she had answered herself, and Cheryl told her no. Her mother reassured her then that it was ok!

Cheryl put the truck in park and then turned the key over. The engine roared back to life. "Yes!"

She put the truck in drive and stepped on the gas. The tires spun uselessly in the ditch, so she put the truck in four-wheel drive.

"Come on, baby!"

She stepped on the gas—a little forward movement but then the tires spun again.

"Fuck! Fuck! Motherfucker!"

She put the truck back in park, got her cell phone out, and dialed Craig. The phone displayed a "no service" message.

"Oh great! Fuck you, phone, and fuck all the nature-loving white spotted owls that prevent cell towers from going up in Adirondack Park!"

She turned off the truck and got out. She was almost at the zigzag turn, more than halfway to Mc-Master Road. She'd have to walk. At least It wasn't too cold, and the wind wasn't blowing.

A grunting noise startled her. She spun around and remembered the deer.

"Oh, and thank you, you fucking stupid deer. I should have run your ass over. You're welcome!"

She turned on her phone's flashlight and started walking. "At least something's working."

She didn't much care for the darkness or the clamor of the woods, especially at night. Her feet made crunching sounds as she walked on top of the snow. An occasional snapping stick noise could be heard off somewhere in the shadows. A voice inside her brain told her not to worry, probably a deer or rabbit. Listening to her own voice brought her comfort.

"Music!" she said. "Let's play some music while we walk."

She looked at her phone and noticed it only had seven-percent battery left. "Perfect! Par for the course. I hate fucking golf, and I hate white spotted owls! I also hate stupid fucking deer!"

She figured she had twenty to thirty minutes of walking to get to her rented house in the sticks. The house her boyfriend convinced her to move into. She would have to use her flashlight sparingly to save the battery.

She heard another grunting noise.

Cheryl stopped. She turned and looked back at the truck, but it was hidden in the gloom.

"What, are you going to keep me company?" She assumed she was having a conversation with a deer, the one that caused her to abandon her vehicle on the side of the road.

The thought of a deer walking with her for the next thirty minutes was comforting. She didn't feel threatened by them, they would never let her get too close. Cheryl didn't hunt. She never considered herself the outdoor type. Cheryl never wanted to stay here, where she grew up. She had planned to move to New York City after high school and attend a fashion design school in Manhattan. Unfortunately, tuition and living expenses were ridiculously expensive and trying to save money with Craig was impossible, especially when he bought ten-year-old used trucks. "Not to mention the shitty thousand-dollar stereo. *Thank you, Craig!*" "*I said, thank you Craig!*"

Another Grunting noise, it seemed closer.

Cheryl looked over to the deer that was still following her. It was still too dark to see. Her brain started weaving together unreasonable scenarios, the kind where she would be attacked by this deer.

She started to laugh. The whole idea was ridiculous.

"Ok, I hear you. Let's go"

They started walking. At least, Cheryl assumed the deer was following her. She couldn't see it, but it wasn't far off. She could hear a second set of footprints crunching in the snow just off to her right. Again, she tried to focus, but everything blended into the darkness. There were two shades of night. Towards the road, it seemed lighter. Approaching the tree line all things were pitch-black.

"Thank youuuu."

Cheryl stopped. The voice had come from in front of her. It sounded like a whisper. A whisper that was loud enough for her to hear.

"Hello, who's there?"

"Thank youuuu, Craaaaaaig."

Cheryl's heart raced as every nightmare, every horror movie she had ever seen, replayed in her mind. Every hair on her body was standing up, and she felt a chill that was not from the cold.

She turned her flashlight on and pointed it up ahead. About 30 feet in front of her was a big buck. He stood impressively, his enormous antlers spread high in the air. It was the biggest deer she had ever seen. The buck didn't look like it was going to charge her. It was just looking at her.

She smiled and relaxed. "It was the fucking wind." She laughed and said to the buck, "Well, I ain't going home with you. Why don't you go hump that slut of a deer that ran me off the road?'"

The big buck started to grin. It slightly opened up its mouth in a creepy approximation of a grin, revealed a frightening set of sharp canines. Suddenly, the darkness crept back into Cheryl's soul. There was no escaping it. This thing was a freak of nature. Her brain started recreating unwanted scenarios. She had a crazy thought that maybe the flash from her camera would scare it off. She lined it up with her phone and pressed the photo button. Just as the flash went off, something hard slammed into Cheryl's side, knocking her to the ground. The phone was jarred loose from her hand, and the wind was knocked out of her. She gasped for air, trying to force her lungs to work again. She pushed herself to one knee and saw what had hit her—another deer stood above her.

"Thank youuuu, Craaaaaaig."

That wasn't the wind? The deer spoke. Her lungs started working, and she filled them with the cold November air. Her breath fogged in front of her as she exhaled. Cheryl got to her feet and looked around for her phone when something else crashed into her, this time from the left. She went down hard. Something cracked in her side. She coughed and tasted the metallic tang of blood. Her breathing became heavy and gurgly. Cheryl was beyond scared now.

She had had enough. She painfully rose to her feet. "Listen, you fucking deer! I'm going to bring back my whole family, every hunter I know, and we are goin' to shoot the fuck out of all of you! Venison for breakfast, lunch and dinn—"

Another deer slammed into her from behind. Her face hit the ground. She rolled over onto her back and felt blood running down her face. She saw stars in her mind. Immediate, intense pain was resonating from her nose. She brought her hand up and felt it, it was definitely busted. Her tongue dragged across a chipped front tooth.

Another grunting noise.

She felt a warm breath on her face, smelling of foul, rotten meat.

"Ouch, you fucking bit me!"

Something had grabbed her left shoulder. She rolled to punch it, but sharp teeth pierced her arm. She started moving. They started dragging her into the woods. Her back scraped painfully against rocks and roots. She had to do something. Cheryl thought of the one person she could always count on. She took in a deep, wet breath and screamed as loud as she could.

"Daddy!"

An echo came back from the woods.

"Daddyyyyyyyyyy. Daddyyyyyyyyyy. Daddyyyyyyyyyy."

Daddy would be the last thought Cheryl ever had.

# CHAPTER SEVEN

# Dad

"Cheryl!"

Sue Peterson's husband shouted so loud; it woke her from her sleep. He screamed so loud; the neighbors must have also woken. Sue reached over to touch her husband, but he was already halfway out of bed with his feet on the floor.

"What is it, Dave?"

"It's Cheryl, she's in trouble!"

# CHAPTER EIGHT

## Encon

Billy was still sleeping when John was about to leave the room. Darrel was already downstairs having breakfast. He was always the first one up. John put shaving cream on Billy's hand and gently rubbed his face with one finger, barely touching the skin. Suddenly, Billy smacked himself, spreading shaving cream in his eyes and up his nose. John could tell right away Billy boy didn't like the taste of it! John slipped out the door, but Billy saw him.

"I'll get you back. Tonight, you'll pay!"

John slammed the door and laughed all the way to the elevator. By the time he reached the dining room, Darrel had finished eating and was on what was probably his third cup of coffee. That was his morning ritual, a light breakfast and several cups of coffee. The others showed up for breakfast about a half-hour later. They all looked to be recovering from a good hangover. Danny was wearing dark sunglasses. Sal was complaining of a headache and Karl was asking everyone to keep the noise down. The TV was on, and Darrel asked the waitress if she could turn the volume up. Karl immediately objected but was overruled by a piercing look from Darrel. The local news had an update on the missing hunter.

"According to Troop B in Ray Brook, the missing hunter is still unaccounted for. Search parties have resumed this morning. In other news, a local named 'Cheryl Peterson' has been reported missing. Her truck was found abandoned on Forest Home Road, and state troopers have initiated an investigation, but as of this moment, they cannot verify weather Miss Peterson is actually missing."

Billy smiled. "Sounds like a certain local girl hooked up with some riff-raff last night!"

"She was probably driving drunk, ditched the truck, and got a ride from some lucky guy!"

Everyone laughed and high-fived each other.

Karl said, "Hey, that's why Sully left the bar so quick last night. He had to go rescue her!"

They laughed even harder, and Sal slapped Karl on the back.

They finished up breakfast and checked out of the Hotel Saranac. Darrel was nostalgic about this place. It was where their parents got married. As he walked down the hallway, he noticed the wallpaper and the carpeting. He wondered what the decor looked like back then, at his parents wedding. He looked at the light fixtures and the doorknobs. There were cheaper places to stay, but Darrel was adamant about staying at "Hot Sara." Some time back, some of the hotel's lights had broken, and the sign read "Hot Sara" instead of "Hotel Saranac." That story always made John smile. The hotel, the name Hot Sara, reminded John of their father.

They stopped at Mobile Mart at the edge of town, to get some last-minute necessities before a week in the woods. Sal grabbed several cans of Kodiak dip, though the stuff made John sick. They filled their five-gallon reserve cans with gas. Karl and John noticed an ECO officer getting a cup of coffee—environmental conservation officer, that is what ECO stood for. Most folks called them ENCONs. This one couldn't have been more than twenty-four.

"How you doin'?" John said.

The officer looked up and nodded. ENCONs weren't as friendly as state troopers—not that the troopers were fun loving guys, but ECONs were usually all business.

John continued with the questions. "Have you been out around Santa Clara lately? Seen any deer?" He scrutinized John for a long time, like the officer was sizing John up for a fight. Then he turned his head toward Karl and started analyzing him.

"Where are you boys from?"

John glanced at Karl and then back at the ENCON guy. Like his father had taught him, John extended his hand and introduced himself. "I'm John Fuller, and this is Karl Davies. We're from Bronxville, just south of White Plains."

The officer shook John's hand but barely smiled. "What's your business out on 458?"

That was the road that ran up through Santa Clara. John knew what he was getting at. He was probably going to follow them out to the vehicles and check for hunting tags, license, and registration. It was buck season. All kills had to be bucks and all kills had to have the proper tag, issued by New York State. Karl was getting nervous. He probably had an ounce of pot in his pocket. He had his hands in his pockets, almost like he was hiding something. Karl was avoiding eye contact and mostly staring down at the floor.

John said, "My family has a hunting camp out that way. Been in the family for three generations."

The officer furrowed his brow. "Whereabouts?"

"Off old Route 72."

Suddenly the ENCON officer's expression changed from all business, to one of approval. "Hey, my partner's got a camp out that way." He looked past them and called another ENCON in the store. "Hey, Phil, come here!"

Phil came, walking over. He was a big dude,

older, maybe in his late thirties, with the same demeanor as his partner—stoic, not real friendly. No facial expression, just a cold hard stare. Now that John thought of it, he didn't even get the first officer's name when they shook hands. All of that didn't matter, John recognized the big guy.

"His family has a hunting camp off 458, off old Route 72," the first officer said.

Phil took a big interest in that. He looked over at John and started smiling. "You know Butch Fuller?"

Before John could respond, Phil wrapped him up in a big bear hug. "How the hell are you Johnnie?"

Phil put him down after a few seconds then looked at Karl like he was no damn good. He then looked back at John and smiled. "I'm sorry to hear about your father's passing."

John didn't say anything back, just looked down at his shoes and nodded.

"Is your brother here?" Phil asked.

John looked up and nodded. "Let me get him." He shouted toward the store. "Moose! Come over here!"

Darrel came over carrying a case of Budweiser. He and Phil made eye contact and smiled.

With exuberance, Phil said, "Little D! You're all growed up!"

They shook hands like long-lost buddies. Phil introduced his partner to everyone. The guy's name was George. Phil told them all about hunting with Butch back in the day. How "Little D" and John tagged along a few times, when they were like ten or eleven. Phil tells the story about a miserable wet day of hunting. They had been out in the woods for hours. The rain never let up, and the ground was saturated. Butch, John's father, was mad at John. John's socks were wet, and he wanted to go home, but it ended with Darrel shooting his first deer—a four pointer.

"How long are you boys going out there?" Phil asked.

Darrel looked at Karl and John. "A week. Have you seen any big guys roaming around?"

Phil looked at George then back at Darrel. "No. To be honest we haven't seen any bucks around for a couple years. A few does, but deer hunting has been miserable the last few years."

"What about Big Charlie?"

Phil and George grinned at each other. "The Martin brothers claim to have seen him a couple weeks back out near Meacham," Phil said. "But I talked to Jeff who said he was spooked by something out there."

John had to ask. "What do you mean spooked?"

George said, "According to the Martins, Big Charlie has sixteen points now."

"What's so spooky about that?"

"Bucks don't get that big up here," Phil said, "They

saw something, but they're being-tight lipped about it. They refuse to go back into the woods. Jeff says he's hanging it up. His hunting days are over. His brother just put his house on—"

"His brother's already gone," George interrupted. His smile had vanished, and he was all business again. "Packed up his family and left the Adirondacks. There is a for sale sign in front of the house."

Phil said, "It's been really strange out here the last couple years. We can't find any more moose anywhere in the park. And, the beavers are gone! It's like they just disappeared."

"Tell them about the rabbits," George said.

Phil nodded. "Yeah, that's strange. We have been getting reports from the local communities about a rabbit infestation."

"A rabbit infestation?" Darrel was puzzled.

George responded, "The rabbits have left the woods and seem to be migrating into the local villages."

"Phil, are you going out to camp this week?" Darrel asked.

"Wish I could Little D. We're too short-handed right now. We've been investigating a missing hunter out near Franklin Falls the last couple days, and now there's another out on Forest Home Road. "John nodded his head and said, "Yeah, we saw the news this morning. Local girl left her truck on the side of the road."

George said, "There's more than that going on out there."

Phil gave him a hard look, apparently telling him to shut up. Then he said, "Well Darrel, it was good catching up with you. Sorry about Butch. I liked him. Gentlemen, it was great meeting you. Hey, Darrel, do you have your radio on you?" Darrel knew what Phil was getting at. There was no cell phone reception out where they were going. The wireless radios allowed them to communicate within a few miles' radius.

"Yes."

"What channel are you boys operating on?"

"Channel 7."

"Ok, if I'm in the area, I'll give you a shout out. Let's go, partner."

George nodded goodbye.

John put his hand on Phil's shoulder and said, "Great seeing you Phil."

Phil smiled back and the two ENCON officers exited the store.

# CHAPTER NINE

## Roadkill

The hunting party finished up getting last-minute essentials and loaded everything into the vehicles. It was about a forty-five-minute ride to the hunting camp. We had just past Paul Smith's College and were cruising on Route 30 just past Barnum Pond. Danny slowed down and pulled over ahead of John. John followed suit. He pulled over so we did too. The Motorola started talking, it was Sal's voice coming through.

"Darrel are you seeing this? Over."

Darrel picked up the walkie talkie.

"See what? Over."

"Pull up to my left side parallel. Over."

Darrel nodded to John, who pulled the SUV alongside their truck.

John wasn't worried about leaving the SUV on the road. There was hardly any traffic. If a car did come, it would have plenty of room to go by. Route 30 branched off into two separate directions a few miles up ahead. John and the boys were not going to Malone, they would be headed to Santa Clara. There was nothing else out here except trees on both sides of the road. It was like they had laid a paved road down in the middle of this forest.

Billy moved in the back seat. "What the Fuck!"

About two-hundred feet off to the right of the road were about five does. They looked to be eating something. Our view was obstructed, their bodies were in the way. Whatever they were grazing on, it was on the other side. Sal and Darrel got out of the vehicles. John pulled ahead and parked on the side of the road. Sal and Darrel approached slowly. They were about one hundred feet away, but the deer kept on grazing. This was alien to John. Deer wouldn't graze like this, not near a major road. And whenever a car approached a deer, it seemed to John they always scattered and ran for cover. They didn't seem to be afraid of the vehicles, or Darrel and Sal approaching them.

Billy and John got out. Danny and Karl did the same, and all carefully approached the scene until they were about sixty feet away. The deer were eating something hungrily. One of the deer looked up from its meal and made eye contact with John.

It had blood on its mouth. The men looked at each other in bewilderment. Sal unholstered a 44 Smith & Wesson, but Darrel gave him a withering look. They each had a tag for one deer—bucks, not does. Sal pointed the gun in the air and pulled the trigger.

*Boom!*

The report was much louder than a regular hunting rifle. The does scattered into the tree line. They were fast, graceful.

"Ouch, you fuck!" Karl said, holding his ears. "Give me a warning next time."

Sal looked at Karl. "You big fucking pussy, go put some pink ear muffins on."

Classic Sal.

They walked closer to have a better look at what the does had been grazing on.

"That's a deer carcass!" Sal said.

Billy shook his head in disbelief and said, "Deer are eating other deer?"

Everyone waited for Darrel to say something. Whenever life became confusing, Darrel was the one they all turned to.

"Roadkill," Darrel said. "They were eating roadkill."

Sal glanced at the road far behind them. "You telling me this carcass was knocked one hundred feet off the road?"

Danny spoke up and said, "It could have been hit by a semi. Or maybe the hit didn't kill it right away and it walked here."

Sal looked over to the road and back to the carcass. "Its kin dragged it. Look at the snow."

Sal pointed at the ground where a trail of bloody drag marks carved a path from the road to the carcass.

Billy looked perplexed. "Why are deer eating deer?"

Darrel tried to make sense of it.

"Deer will eat meat sometimes. They've been known to eat mice or small birds."

"Not their own kind!" Billy spat. "We're talking cannibalism!"

Darrel looked Billy in the eyes. "You heard what Phil said. It's been a long couple years and not a lot of deer have been spotted. Maybe they're starving."

Sal nodded slowly. "So, they're hungry! Yeah. I am too, so let's go get some venison!"

Everyone jumped on board Sal's bandwagon of excitement. Danny and John high-fived each other. Karl hopped on Billy's back. Of course, Sal had to squeeze off three more rounds, firing them loudly into the air. Everyone ran back to the vehicles, and the caravan continued down Route 30.

## CHAPTER TEN

## Black Angus

A few miles up, John and the others caught 458, and fifteen minutes after that, they headed down a dirt road off old Route 72. It was a slow ride from there to the hunting camp as the trucks couldn't go any faster than twenty. The road had too many bumps and potholes, and after November, only a four-wheel drive vehicle could get out there at all.

Ten minutes later, they arrived at the camp. Everyone jumped out to get settled in. Everybody just stood there for a moment, looking at the camp. It was a long one-story structure with a door in the middle. It was made of logs and had two windows on each side of the door. A chimney stack was perched on the roof back toward the left. The gear was put inside and Sal started a fire in the wood stove. It was a crisp twenty degrees outside, but it felt colder inside. Once he got that baby hot, it didn't take long to warm up the cabin.

The camp was nothing elaborate—a rectangular

room of one thousand square feet. There was a big old black wood stove in the corner that doubled as a heater. A propane refrigerator was over by the bar. The bar seemed to be the main hub; it was centered in the room. There were ten wooden stools surrounding it. The shelves behind the bar were mostly empty. A few bottles left from years past. But what caught everyone's attention, was the trophy that hung above the bar. A twelve-point buck named Butch, that John and Darrel's father shot in the early seventies. One of the traditions at camp, was to toast Butch before downing a shot of Maker's Mark. This of course was to honor the hunter who shot the majestic buck that was now the center of attraction at the camp.

Billy didn't waste any time, he quickly restocked the shelves with new bottles of booze and packed the fridge with cold beer. The cabin had three bunk beds and three singles. A few years back, they had fifteen guys in the camp with plenty of space. One of the most important features of the room, was of course, the table. It had been carved out of an old telephone line spindle with the bottom cut out so everyone could comfortably fit their feet. When they weren't hunting, they sat around that table eating and playing cards. The first few days of a hunt, everyone had the best intentions of landing a deer, but as the week lingered on, several hunters usually accepted the fact that they would have better luck at playing cards.

The bathroom was an outhouse outside. It functioned well enough. John remembered when he and Darrel had to build it a few years back. There was an older outhouse, but it had become dilapidated and the trench was almost full. John and Darrel had spent the better part of two days digging a trench by hand. Not fun. It also wasn't fun going to the bathroom in the dark, especially if you were drunk, which they almost always were. Those were the two biggest dangers on the hunt: walking drunk in the dark and Sal with his 44.

Over the next couple hours, everyone settled in for a long week. Darrel's first job was to get the generator up and running. For the first fifteen minutes, everyone was going about their business in the dark. Billy didn't wait for the lights to turn on, he started telling bad jokes. Karl's drinking intensified while Sal and Danny started preparing dinner. The tradition on the first night was cow steak. Sal always brought a huge cooler filled with Busch Light, and Black Angus strip steaks, while Danny cooked up potatoes, onions, and peppers. The two of them argued over how long it took to cook a steak. Eventually the lights did start working and the refrigerator started humming.

John sat down at the bar and took it all in. Billy

slipped him a Maker's Mark neat in a small snifter.

"To Butch." John took a sip, and it tingled with heat as it went down.

Billy poured Karl a Maker's Mark in a shot glass. "To Butch." Karl, of course, chugged his, and looked ready to pass out.

The door opened, and Darrel strode in. He brandished the look of a man who has just accomplished a great task. His second job was spent setting up trail cams in the back. Behind the camp was a trail that led into the woods. Darrel always hung one camera at the fork. The fork was about a quarter mile behind the camp, where the path split in two directions—one east leading to a couple of ponds and the other north-west toward Trombley Landing. Darrel walked over to John, and Billy poured him a Maker's Mark. Billy made a hand gesture towards Karl, who had his head down on the bar. John, Billy, and Darrel then raised their glasses.

John said, "To Butch!"

The three of them downed the Kentucky bourbon. A moment later Billy found their glasses and filled them back up.

Darrel looked over at Sal. "Here's to eating Sal's shitty steak!"

They all drank. Of course, this didn't sit well with Hoss—that's what John's father had called Sal. Hoss was a character from an Old West TV show called,

*Bonanza.* He was a big guy, a gentle giant, stronger than an ox. John had never seen the show, but his father had tried to explain it every year.

Hoss lifted his head up and gave Moose an unpleasant look. "Eat shit and bark at the moon!"

Beer erupted out of Billy's mouth like a hot geyser, he bent over and slapped his leg laughing.

Karl lifted his head off the bar and said, "Good one."

John and Darrel looked at each other and smiled.

Sal then spoke with authority. "These steaks are Black Angus."

Karl raised his hand at the bar and said, "Why is it black?"

That stumped everyone for a moment.

Sal became impatient and raised his voice another octave. "It doesn't matter what they call it. It tastes good!"

They all drank to that. After dinner and a few more beers, they started talking. The conversation started with Billy and his girlfriend. She wanted a ring, but he wasn't ready for that kind of a commitment. Billy kept going on and on about it. Darrel finally told him to shut the fuck up and grow a pair! Sal said he was thinking of quitting his job and doing something else. His uncle was an ironworker and he told Sal he could probably get him in the union. Danny was seriously thinking about enlisting in the Navy. This wasn't news to them, he had mentioned it a couple years ago. One by one, each of them shared. They did this every year. It was like going to counseling. You were safe among people you trusted.

Suddenly, Karl threw a curve ball. "What the fuck is really going on up here?"

The camaraderie crept away, and the room became silent. Everyone knew exactly what he meant, but no one wanted to talk about it.

Darrel looked at Karl like he was from another planet. Karl got annoyed. He started pointing his finger at Darrel. "That kid, on the poster, he's gone. The missing hunter. Sully and his story. Phil telling us about the rabbits and beavers!"

Billy twitched. He always did when he got nervous. "What about the rabbits and beavers?

Karl looked at Billy and said, "The ENCON guy Phil, he said there are no more rabbits or beavers left in the Adirondacks."

Sal said, "Well I could've told ya that. We saw, what, maybe two girls in town yesterday!"

Everyone laughed except Karl.

"What about the cannibalistic deer?"

Darrel looked at Karl, like he was annoyed with him. "Well, what's your theory?"

Karl looked back at Darrel. "I say we get up in the morning and go home!"

They were stunned. Sal stood suddenly, knocking his chair to the floor behind him. "No way. You know how hard it is for me to get time off to come up here with you guys? You're more than welcome to start walking, but this is my vacation for the year! I'm staying!"

Danny brought both hands up and started shaking them. "What the fuck Karl? You can't be serious?"

Karl looked over at his lifelong friend. "Danny, this doesn't feel right! Something's wrong up here."

Sal said, "Everyone just relax. Let's get a good night's sleep."

Darrel looked at Karl. "Hey, we got your back. We have more weapons and ammo here than Fort Drum!"

Sal laughed and raised his 44. "And I got my cannon!"

Billy poured Karl a Maker's Mark and brought it over.

"Enough of this bullshit." Sal changed the subject. "It's time for a little Texas Holdem."

He sat down and shuffled the cards. The others took their seats at the table. Darrel was last to sit down. "I got no problem taking your money, but we're all getting up early."

"Ok, Dad!" Sal said with a sarcastic sulk.

The others jumped on board.

"Yes, sir!"

"Will you read me a bedtime story, Moose?"

"Early to bed, Dad!"

John laughed too hard to pile on.

Finally, Darrel stopped the verbal attacks. "Just deal the fucking cards."

There was a momentary silence, and then they all started up again.

"Can I have a glass of water Dad!"

"I need my blankie Dad."

"Read me Winnie the Pooh, please."

The laughter started echoing off the walls of the camp. John stood up from the table, he was trying to say something, but his laughter suppressed the words from coming out. Finally, Darrel smiled and shook his head as the cards were dealt.

# CHAPTER ELEVEN

---

# *Troop B*

Troop B in Ray Brook was swamped. They were in the middle of processing a DWI and investigating a lost hunter and a missing woman out on Forest Home Road, and they were holding two locals for assault. Phil and his partner George were in a meeting with Major Vierra, Troop B's commander. Lieutenant Johnson from the Bureau of Criminal Investigation and troopers Williams and Sprague were also present while Lieutenant Johnson briefed the Major on his investigation.

"Still not found. We're going to bring the other guys in from the hunting party and re-question them."

The Major asked, "Was there any evidence of foul play?"

Lieutenant Johnson said, "There were a lot of tracks, and it looked like something was dragged. We didn't find any footprints. Definitely deer, possibly coyote.

Major Vierra looked confused? "What do you mean 'dragged'?"

"We found what looked like heel marks from boots and someone lying on their back. We dragged Trooper Mortenson on his back for about ten yards for comparison. The pattern in the snow looked similar."

The major looked at the Lieutenant for a long time. "How many troopers did it take to drag Mortenson?"

"Three of us, sir."

The major had a blank stare for a few seconds, like he was doing some calculating. He knew the size of Trooper Mortensen, big guy, over two hundred and fifty pounds. "How much did the missing hunter weigh?"

"According to his buddies, Mr. Callfield was around two-hundred pounds."

The Major looked over at Phil and George. "What can drag a two-hundred pound man?"

George put his hand in the air like he was in grade school. "A black bear, sir. It's really the only predator that's strong enough."

The major looked at Phil like he knew that the senior ENCON officer would have a better explanation.

"I think we may have a new predator making its way into the Adirondacks," Phil said. "I think it could be a mountain lion."

"A mountain lion? You're talking about a cougar! How big can those predators get?"

"Anywhere from five to nine feet long and up to two hundred and twenty-five-pounds."

The major was stunned.

Phil continued, "We looked at the cell phone pictures from the missing girl out on Forest Home Road. I think it backs up my hypothesis."

The major looked at Trooper Williams. "I want to see the pictures off that phone."

"I just need a minute to pull them up."

Williams opened the laptop and flipped on the overhead projector.

While he searched for the files, Phil continued explaining his theory. "A black bear would be sleeping by now, and the ones that aren't are trying to find a den. Black bears are opportunistic, they'll eat roadkill, but they won't risk their life, especially when humans are involved."

"What if the black bear was rabid?" George said. "That could explain its behavior."

Trooper Williams looked up at Major Vierra. "Ready sir."

Vierra looked up at the board to see a massive buck staring back at him. "That has to be over three hundred pounds. Is that fourteen points?"

"Sixteen, sir!"

The major looked over at Phil. "Ok, it's a big

buck. Biggest one I have ever seen. Where's the mountain lion?"

Phil walked up to the board and pointed at the deer's eyes. "He's not looking at the camera. He sees something off to the left. I think this buck was being chased causing Miss Peterson to lose control of her truck and become stuck on the side of the road. She got out and started walking toward McMaster Road where she rents a house with her boyfriend. Then she got jumped by this mountain lion."

The Major nodded. "Do you have any other evidence of the mountain lion?"

George said, "We lifted two types of tracks. One was definitely deer, but the other was a large predator."

The lieutenant spoke up next.

"We found two sets of tracks in our investigation also."

The major then asked, "Can someone be more specific. Was it a mountain lion print, or something else?"

"It's not a bear track and it's bigger than a cougar track," Phil responded.

The major looked at Lieutenant Johnson. The lieutenant nodded his head in agreement with Phil.

The major looked confused. "How far is it from Franklin Falls to Forest Home Road?"

"About ten miles. That's not far for a big cat to go in twenty-four hours."

The major sat back in his chair. "Sometimes I hate this job. I have to go tell the girl's father that his daughter has been eaten by a mountain lion?"

No one had an answer.

"Her father's being held three rooms down," the major said. "We arrested him for beating the crap out of his daughter's boyfriend. He believes her boyfriend is involved with her disappearance."

The major stood up and became stoic. "We're keeping a lid on this mountain lion speculation until we get more proof. If we don't have anything else in twenty-four hours, we'll leak our theory to the press. Dismissed."

# CHAPTER TWELVE

## Game Cam

The card game wrapped up around two in the morning. Sal won a couple hundred dollars, beating Danny on the river card to win the final pot. Danny had a full house, jacks over fives, but Sal pulled the three of diamonds on the river and won with a straight flush. They'd played for bigger pots, but it was still fun, especially the way Sal did it. Even Danny had laughed and shook his head. It was early in the week, after all. There was still plenty of time for Danny to win his money back. A good night's sleep in hunting camp amounted to four or five hours if you were lucky. John woke up when the door opened. It was Darrel. He had a game cam in hand. The camera was designed to be used in an outdoor environment. It is motion activated and when triggered, it snaps a picture. John got up and walked over to the stove where he smelled the strong aroma of coffee and poured himself a cup. Darrel must have been really quiet when he got up this morning. John and the others hadn't even woken up. John strolled over to the table. Darrel had just sat down and was hooking the camera up to his laptop.

"Thanks for making coffee."

Darrel nodded and said, "You guys weren't moving this morning."

John asked, "Where's that one from?"

"By the fork."

A minute after he hooked it up, pictures started uploading to the laptop.

John pointed at one of the images. "Is that a coyote?"

Darrel nodded. The next few images were blurry, but the fourth showed four deer running past the camera, including one massive buck.

"Jackpot!" Darrel shouted.

The others jumped out of bed and stumbled over.

"Big Charlie's alive and well," Darrel said. The buck's body was blurred, but his rack and size were unmistakable.

Danny got up and headed to the stove. "Come on, Karl. Let's get breakfast going."

Danny and Karl always cooked breakfast—usually scrambled eggs with bacon, green peppers, onions, and potatoes topped with shredded mozzarella. They then wrapped it all up in a soft tortilla shell. Hoss called them "hunting camp breakfast burritos."

Billy skipped back to the table with his plate. "I'm getting that bastard!"

"A hog's ass you are!" Hoss said. "That buck is mine."

Darrel closed up his laptop while the rest of them got dressed.

# CHAPTER THIRTEEN

## Bill's Big Buck

Twenty minutes later, they were fed and geared up to go buck hunting. It was a brisk November morning. The sun would be up in an hour.

Darrel got everyone's attention. "OK, this is how it's going down. Billy and I will be at the fork. Hoss and Danny will be two-hundred yards east."

Karl blurted, "Why do I always have to be the spooker?"

Sal said, "Because I'm too fat you skinny little bastard!"

The others laughed. Sal had a point. The spooker had to get the deer that had bedded down up and moving. When a deer got spooked, it would ideally walk in front of the spotters, who were lying in wait, guns loaded and at the ready.

"No," Karl said. "I have to spook first every year."

Darrel ignored him. "Johnnie you and Karl will start when I give the Tom call."

The Tom call was a turkey gobble. Darrel was

good at it. Many times, he could get actual turkeys to approach him.

They agreed to the plan and walked into the woods. It took us about five minutes to get to the fork and another five to get into position. The set-up was a long shot. The deer from the trail cam were probably long gone. But they expected a long day in the woods, and it was worth the easy thirty minutes for the chance that Big Charlie might walk in front of their rifles.

A loud warble came from Darrel's direction, so Karl and John started walking. It was a twenty-minute loop. They started at the fork and passed Darrel and Billy. They didn't even know they were there until Billy said hello from behind the trees. About five minutes later they passed by Sal and Danny. The two of them were hidden well. They only knew it was them because they could hear Hoss whispering to Danny to shut the fuck up. Finally, they circled back toward the fork.

———

It had been about ten minutes since John and Karl spooked by. Darrel and Billy rested comfortably behind a tree about thirty feet from the path. Darrel was holding his father's 1970 .30-30 lever-action Winchester. He owned a better rifle than this—a four-year-old .30-6 with a high-powered scope. Darrel had tagged three bucks with it in the past, but today, he was going with the nostalgic factor. His father had already planned to hand down the rifle as a rite of passage, but nobody had expected the heart attack.

Billy was sporting a brand-new Savage Model 110, compliments of his girlfriend. She forked over one thousand dollars for it. It still smelled like it was right out of the box. Darrel could tell Billy was proud of it. Billy kept staring at it. He barely noticed their surroundings. If a buck walked out in front of him, he wouldn't even be interested. Darrel was sure Billy would be afraid to fire his new rifle. He might scuff it up.

"Are you going to give that back to her when she dumps your ass?" Darrel whispered.

"A big fuck you to my good buddy, Moose!"

Suddenly, three rabbits ran by on the path, followed by a fox and two more rabbits. Darrel had never seen rabbits and foxes running together. A deer popped out of the brush, causing one of the trailing rabbits to leap a little higher. The deer snatched the rabbit out of the air. It shook its head violently and clamped its jaws down on the rabbit. *Snap!* The crunch of the rabbit's bones breaking paralyzed Darrel. The doe disappeared into the brush, the rabbit in its mouth.

Suddenly, they heard something headed their way. It was moving fast and making a lot of noise—definitely not human. It sounded like a deer running in the woods. Darrel and Billy readied their rifles. A moment later, a big ten-point buck walked out of the brush and stopped in the middle of the path. If they didn't hear it coming, they would've missed it. The buck blended in with the surrounding topography. If they were farther away, it would've been hard to spot against the backdrop of the brush and trees. It was breathing hard, like it had been running for a while. It glanced back, tail in the air like it was nervous.

The buck turned and looked right where Darrel was, almost like it sensed his presence. Darrel hesitated on the trigger. Something had spooked this buck, and he was certain it wasn't Karl or John.

Billy didn't wait any longer, *Pow!*

The buck staggered two steps and dropped.

"Yeah, baby!"

Billy ran out to inspect the kill. It was a good shot, clean. Billy had hit the buck in the upper shoulder. The big fella was dead before he hit the ground.

Sal's voice chirped on the Motorola. "Did we get one? Over!"

Darrel responded,

"Yeah, Billy just dropped a ten pointer! Over."

John and Karl were about fifteen minutes into their spooking when they heard the sound of gunfire. One shot. Didn't sound like Darrel's .30-30. Then they heard Darrel on the radio—Billy had dropped a ten pointer.

Karl was pissed. "Lucky bastard. That was my buck. I have to spook every year."

John grinned at him.

"Come on, it's the first day out! There's still time. Anyway, that's the first buck Billy's shot since he was fifteen."

Karl laughed. "Ya, he was due!"

When they rejoined the others, Billy was doing an Irish jig. Sal was telling him to hurry up and field dress it and Danny was calling Billy a lucky fucker!

Darrel was a few feet back just staring off into the brush.

"What's spooking you big brother?" John asked.

Darrel looked at John. "Have you ever seen a deer catch a rabbit before?"

John thought about that and shook his head.

"Well apparently you can add rabbit to the list of animals deer eat." Darrel explained how Billy and he witnessed a deer catch a rabbit. John was having problems comprehending his brother's story. He wondered if the two of them, Darrel and Billy, were still drunk. Probably a tall tale they concocted to spin a rouge over everyone. But at the end of his story, John noticed that his brother was dead serious about the whole thing. He was just dumb struck how Billy got the shot off before Darrel. Out of all of them, Darrel was the best shot.

A few minutes later, Sal was talking Billy through gutting the deer. "Stop right deer. I mean there! You even nick the stomach or bladder, we're screwed!"

Billy had dressed a deer before, but it had been—several years. After about twenty minutes, the entrails were piled up nicely on the ground outside the stomach cavity. Billy tied a couple of loops under the front legs and around the antlers, then he tied the rope to a stick. Billy started dragging the buck, but Sal pushed him down.

"Get out of the way you big pussy."

Sal threw the buck over his shoulders and walked back towards the cabin. The others shrugged and followed.

Billy pushed himself off the ground. "Wait for me!"

An hour later, Billy's buck was hung up draining outside, while the hunters were inside drinking. Sal had cut the backstraps out and prepared them for supper. Billy was adamant that his ten pointer should be hung up next to Butch. This didn't sit well with Darrel and John. They both agreed Billy's buck should be hung in the outhouse. Karl kept calling Billy a lucky fucker. The Maker's Mark started flowing and Butch was toasted to, several times. They planned to go back out and hunt the rest of the day, but one shot led to two, and then two led to three. After about an hour, most of them had fallen asleep for a mid-day-siesta. Everyone was sure Moose would be the first one to wake up. So, he promised to get them all up in a few hours. It was a tradition to always have drinks before dinner, at hunting camp.

# CHAPTER FOURTEEN

## Something is on the Roof

John was in a deep sleep when suddenly he woke up to the sound of Sal's voice. He couldn't quite make out what Sal said, but noticed Darrel looking up at the ceiling. Then John heard it, like something was walking on the roof. It sounded like a big dog walking on a sidewalk. The click-clack noise it made when its paws tapped down against the cement. John then realized that it was bigger than a dog. He could tell from the steps it was taking. It sounded bigger—much bigger.

"What the fuck is that?"

Billy was up, too. He stood up and walked toward where the sounds were coming from, watching the ceiling the whole time.

Darrel noticed Sal pointing his cannon at the ceiling and said, "Don't do it!"

Sal ignored him and kept his cannon aimed at the noise above his head.

A moment later, it sounded like it jumped off, landed on the ground, and trotted away.

"My buck?" Billy ran for the door. Danny, Sal, and John followed him. By the time they got out there, Billy was already swearing at God.

The buck was gone. The rope was still tied to the post, but the other end and the buck were missing. Danny was holding the end of it and said, "Something gnawed it in half."

John said, "It must not have been hung too tight."

Everyone looked around for clues. There was less than an hour of daylight left, and the sun was partially hiding behind the clouds.

Danny was pointing to tracks. "Looks like something dragged the buck off into the woods over here."

Billy ran over to see. "What dragged it off into the woods.?" He looked at Danny in disbelief. "Did we even get a fucking picture? Come on, tell me someone got a picture of my buck!"

Billy stared at the drag marks leading into the woods. "Let's go get my buck back!"

Darrel looked up at the sky. "We got about thirty minutes of daylight left. I say we go back inside and regroup."

"Regroup? I say we go find the motherfucker who took my buck and end his life with Hoss's cannon!"

Karl said, "I say we go inside, pack our bags, and go home!" There was an uncomfortable silence for a brief moment. Karl was looking down at his feet, like he didn't dare to look anyone in the eyes.

"Karl has a point."

Everyone looked at Danny. He kept turning his head from the cabin, to the woods. He didn't look very comfortable standing this close to the edge of the woods.

"There are some strange things going on out here," Danny said. "Come on, can someone tell me what was walking on top of the roof?"

"Listen," Sal said, pulling Billy into a bear hug, "we have some amazing back straps from your buck. They didn't take that from us!  Before we decide anything, let's go back inside and eat some venison."

Everyone jumped on the idea and went back inside. After a round of venison steaks, they all sat down at the table. Dinner was awkward, there wasn't much conversation. Everybody was hoping for someone to speak, but nobody was in a hurry to break the silence.

"It had to be a bear," Sal said. "It would be strong enough to lift it off the hanger and drag it into the woods."

Danny and Billy nodded in agreement.

Darrel spoke up and said, "Those don't look like bear tracks out there."

Sal picked up a can of Busch Light, making it disappear in his massive hand. He drank the remainder with one guzzle. A loud belch echoed out of his chest. "Well what do you think dragged a two-hundred pound deer into the woods, not to mention lifting it up off the hanger, Moose?"

Darrel didn't look at Sal. Instead, he looked up at the ceiling. Then he turned his gaze to include everyone at the table. "When you start adding everything up, I'm starting to agree with Karl. I mean, think about what we've seen up here the last couple days. Missing boy posters, missing hunter in the woods, Sully's story, and the missing girl."

No one said a thing.

"Now, this happens. Billy, that was a great buck you got, buddy."

"Thank you, Moose."

Darrel looked at Billy for a moment. "That should have been my kill. I saw it for a good three to five seconds, just like you. I could have pulled the trigger first, but I didn't. I hesitated."

Everyone had trouble processing the thought of Darrel hesitating to shoot a ten-point buck. Sal looked like he wanted to say something, but he didn't. Karl, Billy, Danny and John all just stared at Darrel.

"Tell them what we saw before your buck came out Bill."

Billy looked confused and then the light came back to his face. "Craziest thing. Rabbits and a fox running down the path together like something's chasing them. Then this doe jumps out from the woods and snatches a rabbit in midair with its mouth. It chomps down and kills it then goes back into the woods."

"What did it do with the rabbit?'

Billy looked at Danny with a twisted face. "Ate it? I don't fucking know!"

Sal said, "I've never seen a deer hunt rabbits!"

Karl raised his hand.

"Apparently, they also eat roadkill," said Karl.

John thought about everything that had happened. "Maybe they know how to climb and walk on top of hunting camps?"

Darrel looked over at Karl. "How much do you weigh?"

Karl noticed everyone looking at him, like he did something wrong. He was annoyed by the sudden attention. His facial muscles started to tense up like a boxer anticipating a jab to the jaw. "About one hundred and seventy-pounds."

Darrel looked around at everyone. "If a two-hundred pound, ten-point buck can be dragged off into the woods that quickly, then it's not safe for us to be out here."

For a long time, everyone stayed silent. Billy was staring out the window, where his buck had been hanging. Karl was looking at the floor. Danny and

John were looking at each other, and they were both shaking their heads in disbelief. Finally, Sal said, "So what you're saying is we have a pack of deer running around the Adirondacks and hunting people?"

"Fuck me!" Billy stood up and knocked his chair over backwards.

"This sounds like science fiction crap to me. I'm not buying it!" Said Danny.

Suddenly, the wireless radio crackled to life. "Little D are ya there? Over."

It was Phil. Darrel picked up.

"Hey Phil, what's up? Over."

"I want to advise you of a potential threat out in the woods. We might have a big predator out there. Mountain lion. We haven't confirmed it yet. Over."

Darrel looked at everyone and silently mouthed "mountain lion."

"We just had a ten pointer-jacked," he said into the radio. "We had it hanging up outside, and it's gone. Over."

"How big was the buck? Over."

"About two hundred pounds. Over."

There was a pause as Phil likely processed this information. "Sounds like you boys have a problem out there. Over."

"Phil, what do you recommend we do? Over."

"Stay there tonight," Phil said. "Pack up your gear and get out of their first light tomorrow. Don't let anyone walk off alone. Over."

"Thanks, Phil. Over."

"Be safe, Over and out."

Darrel looked around at everyone.

"Well, at least we know what was walking on top of the roof."

Over the next several hours, the hunting party was consumed by cards and alcohol, an occasional bad joke, and walks down memory lane. The final poker hand came down to Karl and Sal. Karl had a straight. Sal had ten high, but Sal went all in. Karl was still crisp from the previous night's loss, so he folded the winning hand. Of course, Sal had to show everyone that ten high could beat a straight, and much laughter ensued. Karl wasn't laughing. He sat there and pierced Sal with a vengeful stare. Like he was measuring the moment and scheming at the same time. He got up and walked toward Sal. Sal tensed up, he was preparing for some kind of retaliation and Karl looked pissed. Everyone else watched with great anticipation, highly expecting Karl to go on the offense. When Karl got to Sal, he farted really loud. This caused the room to explode in laughter. It took a while for everyone to settle down.

John had a smile on his face, but deep down in his soul, he was troubled. There was something wrong up here in these mountains. In the morning, they would go home.

# CHAPTER FIFTEEN

## Wake Up Karl

The smell of coffee got John out of bed. It was still dark out; sunrise would happen within the hour. The rest rolled out over the next fifteen minutes except Karl. He'd had too much to drink the night before, and not even a mountain lion was going to wake him up. Nobody cooked breakfast; the plan was to stop for breakfast in Keene Valley. There was a good diner they always ate at when leaving the Adirondacks.

Five of them sat at the table. Danny was nice enough to pack up Karl's stuff.

"When the sun comes up, let's pack up the vehicles and shut this place down." Darrel wasn't in a hurry to go out behind the camp and unhook the generator in the dark.

Sal said, "They say mountain lions have been known to stalk hikers for days. You always hear about people being attacked out west in the Rockies."

"I think you mean in Yellowstone." John corrected.

"Or maybe out in the Sierra Nevada's."

Sal looked at John. "If you say so Einstein."

Suddenly, Karl broke wind. He farted so loud and so long that everyone started laughing and couldn't stop. Billy fell backwards off his chair, which caused even more laughter.

"Will you guys shut the fuck up!" Karl grumbled. "Go to sleep!"

Sal shouted back, "Hey, numb nuts, we're leaving in ten minutes. Get your ass moving!"

"Shut up and go back to bed. Give me one more hour."

Sal flashed an evil grin. Poor Karl was about to get Hoss's wrath. Sal walked over to Karl's bed, pulled down his pants and stuck his ass in Karl's face. When a plus-size, three-hundred pound man breaks wind a few inches from your face, the results are catastrophic. Sal ripped a loud one—not as long as Karl's, but wet. The laughter became all the louder.

"You fucker! Get the fuck away from me!" Every muscle in Karl's face was contracting at the same time. He had a total look of disgust.

Sal backed off two steps, but his pants were around his ankles, and he tripped. This caused more uncontrollable laughter. Even Karl cracked a smile.

"Ok, I'm up. Give me ten minutes and I'll be ready." Karl looked down at Sal. "Pull your pants up and stick a cork in your ass!"

More laughter started to reverberate off the walls. Wearing his classic red union suit, Karl slid his boots on and headed for the outhouse, slamming the cabin door behind him.

Danny snorted. "After that record breaker, Karl probably needs more than ten minutes!"

Our laughter was cut short by a blood-curdling scream outside.

"Get the fuck off me!" Karl shouted. "Argh! Let go!"

Darrel was the first to the door followed by Billy and Danny.

"Help! Help meeeeeee!"

Karl's screams were fading. It was still dark outside, and the others couldn't see him.

"Over there!" Darrel pointed toward the woods. They could faintly see something moving in that direction. "It's Karl!"

They ran toward him as he screamed, "Darrel, help!"

The screams became distant, lost in the woods.

Darrel looked at John. "Johnnie, you and Danny grab the guns."

Darrel and Billy ran off in the direction of Karl's screams.

"Let's go!" Sal said. He already had our rifles in hand. He tossed John his Remington 700 and handed another one to Danny. The three of them headed into the woods after the others.

They ran as fast as they could in the brush, stumbling over tree roots, stumps, and fallen branches in the dark. Darrel and Billy weren't far up ahead.

"Karl! Karl, where are you buddy?" They recognized Darrel's voice.

Karl's voice came faintly in the distance, "Help! Over here!"

The voice came from off to the right.

"This way!" Darrel said, running in the direction of Karl's voice.

The others turned to follow. Tree branches and bushes slapped John in the face. He threw up a hand to hold them back.

"Help me!" Karl was closer now, west of their position.

They turned to follow, their pace quickening. There was less brush in that direction, and the sun began to brighten the horizon.

"Karl? Karl, we are coming buddy." Sal shouted.

Sal was steadfast, but doubt was starting to creep in. John could see it in his face. Darrel and Billy were about a hundred feet ahead now. John imagined Karl being mauled by a mountain lion, and he forced his legs to work harder, closing the distance.

"Help meeeeeeee!"

Everyone stopped. John made eye contact with Darrel, who was not that far away now.

"Karl, scream something!" Darrel looked nervous.

Danny and Sal caught up, out of breath. Sal, in particular, wasn't built to run long distances.

"Here." Sal tossed Darrel's rifle to him and handed another to Billy.

"Help meeeeeeee!"

Everyone's head turned. The voice came from behind them this time.

"Over here!" Said Sal. He ran, while the rest followed. "Keep screaming Karl."

They were headed back towards the cabin. With a burst of speed, Darrel ran past Sal to the front, with John and Billy just behind.

"Keep going," Sal huffed as the others passed him. "I'll catch up."

# CHAPTER SIXTEEN

# Never Run from a Fight

Sal slowed down, out of breath, while the others ran ahead. He took a knee and tried to slow his breathing down. He didn't mind being on his knee, it reminded him of when he was a defensive tackle. He loved tackling people—shoving the offensive linemen, throwing them out of the way to make the tackle on a pretty boy running back.

Sal looked around. He was in a small clearing, surrounded by a thicket of hobblebush and honeysuckle. The morning sun was up. His thoughts were directed to Karl. He was overwhelmed with the thought of his good buddy being attacked by a cougar. Sal started praying to God. "Please let Karl be ok. I know I haven't always believed in you, but Karl doesn't deserve this."

Sal's conversation with God was suddenly interrupted. The biggest buck he had ever seen appeared about 40 feet in front of him. It just walked out of a thicket like it had been swimming in the stuff. Sal made eye contact with it, and the thing seemed to grin at him. It had a massive rack. Sal reached down and pulled his cannon from his holster, and started to raise it. Out of the blue, another animal slammed into him, knocking him on his side. His .44 fell to the ground. Sal rolled to his feet and saw it was another deer.

The big buck still had the same grin on its face. Sal looked to his right, where the previous deer had gone. He anticipated that it would attack him once more, but instead, he got blasted from the left again by a second deer. He fell over and landed on his chest. He lifted his head just as it ran off into the underbrush. Sal's face started turning red, he had never run from a fight in his life.

Sal looked at the big buck and said, "OK, let's play!"

He got to his knees and pulled out his knife. It was big, designed for field dressing an enormous buck. Sal fine-tuned his ears to listen for a certain sound. The kind of sound a deer made when it moved in the woods. He heard a noise coming from behind. He sensed another attack and dove just as the creature jumped out of the bush behind him. He thrust his knife up and caught the deer under the chest in its belly. Momentum drove the deer forward as Sal pulled his knife out. He ripped a long gash in the underbelly. Sal instantly felt warm blood, and other liquids saturate his hand. The animal made a moaning noise and took a few steps forward, and then fell to the ground.

Sal didn't wait for the next attack. He scurried over and grabbed his .44. Still on his knees, with his knife in one hand and his cannon in the other, Sal looked at the big buck, still standing there.

"That all you got?"

Before he could say another word, another deer came at him from the right.

*Boom!*

The cannon hit its mark, and the deer went down hard a few feet from where Sal knelt.

Sal stood up, "I can do this all day, mother fucker!"

Movement from his left. Sal turned and fired off another round.

*Boom!*

The bullet hit the oncoming deer right in the middle of its forehead. Blood and bone fragments hit Sal in the face. He tried to rub them off when he suddenly got slammed into by the big buck. Antlers pierced his chest, neck, and face. He felt immense pressure against his left eye as his body was lifted up off the ground. The buck drove Sal's full three-hundred pounds back, crushing him against a tree. His left eye went black, he could feel fluid drip down his face. The wind was knocked out of his lungs. With his remaining eye, Sal watched as the massive buck disengaged, pulling its antlers from his body. Sal gasped for air while the buck took two steps backwards and grunted. Then, it reared up on its hind legs and let out a scream unlike anything Sal had ever heard.

Sal covered his ears. It dropped to the ground and stepped closer, raising its front leg where a sharp claw protruded from its hoof. It brought the hoof down sharply, eviscerating Sal's midsection in three slices.

Sal breathed again, but he was bleeding out. His knife was on the ground. He lifted his cannon, but it wasn't there—the .44 lay on the ground as well, out of reach.

Sal reached in his shirt breast pocket and pulled out a can of Kodiak. He opened the tin and put half the chew in his mouth, packing it in his left cheek and squeezing the juice into his mouth.

"Nice one," he said.

That old familiar feeling started to glaze over, Sal felt a buzz coming on. He looked up at his angel of death. It still had that grin on its face.

"You're not a bear or a cougar. You're just ugly!"

He spat tobacco juice at the big bastard, hitting the buck's foot. Instinctively, the buck stepped back and grunted.

Sal raised his hand like a gun, pulled his thumb like a trigger, and said, "Fuck you!"

The big buck grinned a little wider, exposing an array of sharp teeth, like a carnivore, Sal thought.

Then to Sal's surprise, the buck spoke. "Fuck youuuuuuuu!"

# CHAPTER SEVENTEEN

# Danny Boy

John was in a full sprint. He passed Billy until he and Darrel pulled away from the rest.

*Boom!* It was Sal's cannon. John and Darrel stopped running. Billy and Danny caught up a few seconds later.

"Maybe he found Karl," Billy said.

Darrel nodded at Billy, and everyone turned around and headed back to where they had left Sal. They were exhausted. Danny tripped on a stump and fell down.

"Get up Danny," John said.

"Let's go Danny," Darrel shouted.

Danny struggled to get to his feet as fast as he could, he was now bringing up the rear. The thought of seeing Karl next to Sal made John go faster. He even laughed a little, under his breath, thinking of how Sal had woken Karl with his ass that morning.

*Boom!*

Another shot, definitely Sal's .44. Why would he fire two rounds? A .44 slug could easily stop a black bear. Darrel and John took the lead again. A deafening animal howl filled the woods, they stopped in their tracks. Darrel and John made eye contact.

"That wasn't a human scream," said John.

"And that didn't sound like a cougar," Said Darrel.

They ran faster, not waiting for Danny and Billy to catch up.

They found Sal a few minutes later, learning against a tree in a small clearing. Three dead deer spread out around him.

"What did you do Hoss?"

Darrel was surveying the scene, he hadn't noticed the shape Sal was in, but John did. He was smashed up badly. His stomach was torn up, and there was a lot of blood spilling out of him. Sal had a nasty gash on his cheek, and he was missing an eye.

"You can't just shoot any deer! We only have tags for bucks." Darrel was looking at the three deer that Sal had killed. He was shaking his head in a disapproving way.

"He's gone." John said.

Darrel looked up at John and noticed his brother pointing at Sal.

Danny and Billy showed up next. They saw that John had tears flowing down his cheeks.

"John, what's going on?" Said Billy.

Billy looked over at Sal where Darrel was standing over him. Something was wrong. Darrel was crying. That's when we all realized, Sal was dead.

"Help meeeeeeee!"

Billy looked up. "It's Karl! He's still alive!"

Darrel shook his head no.

"Come on, we have to save him," said Danny.

Darrel looked up at Billy and Danny, then back to John. "It's not him!"

Billy looked at Darrel in disbelief.

Karl's voice came again. "Help meeeeeeee!"

Billy and Danny turned toward the sound and started running. John looked at Darrel, shrugged, and followed them. They seemed to be heading back toward the camp, but John wasn't sure. His mind raced. He heard Darrel close behind him.

"Help meeeeeeee!"

They all stopped. It came from a different direction, east of their location.

"This way," Darrel said.

Darrel took the lead again with John at his heels. More thickets of bramble bushes. They were pulling away from Danny and Billy. Darrel ran like he was possessed. He was separated from John, breathing hard.

John couldn't stop. He didn't hear the others behind him, but he could still see Darrel. A few minutes later, he caught up to him at the fork.

"What's up?" John said, barely getting the words out as he gasped for air. Darrel was just standing there, listening. Billy came up behind, bending over to catch his breath.

"Why'd you st— "

"Shut up and listen!" Darrel snapped.

We became quiet. Thirty seconds passed, but it felt like an hour. John's breathing started to settle. There was no wind. The clouds moved to block the sun, and a light snow began to fall. Soon, the ground would be wet. Leaves wouldn't crunch under hunters' feet. Easy to sneak up on an unsuspecting deer. Perfect hunting conditions.

Suddenly, Darrel looked at Billy. "Where's Danny?"

"He was right behind me!"

Everyone looked back where we came from. Darrel walked into the brush and screamed, "Danny! Danny!"

We followed. Darrel broke into a run.

"Danny!"

"Danny boy!"

"Danny, where are you?"

Another thought crept into John's mind. They were no longer concerned for Karl. Their focus was on Danny now. John jogged past Billy. His energy was utterly spent, but he kept going. Darrel was just up ahead, still calling out Danny's name.

# CHAPTER EIGHTEEN

## "Help Meeeeeee"

"Danny, where the fuck are you?" Billy started crying. He couldn't comprehend that Karl got attacked by a cougar. That Sal was dead, and where was Danny? He had to stop to catch his breath. John disappeared into the woods ahead of him. He would have to catch up. He needed to collect himself just for one minute.

He thought of Sal, and tears flowed more. How his own big mouth would get him in trouble and Sal was always there to save him from getting his ass kicked. He remembered how funny Sal was. He couldn't stop them. He sat down, and set his rifle down, brought his knees up to his chest, and covered his face with hands. His crying became wailing. This couldn't be happening. It must be a bad dream. Any second now, he would open his eyes and wake up in his bed with Sal's ass in his face. Billy laughed at the thought.

Then he heard the wind whisper. "Help meeeeeeee!"

Billy lifted his face up from his hands and saw a deer about twenty feet in front of him.

"Help meeeeeeee!" That time from a different direction.

He turned to the left. There was another deer, staring at him.

"Help meeeeeeee!"

Two more appeared to his right. They walked slowly toward him.

"Help meeeeeeee!"

The voice was behind him. Billy could feel its breath on the back of his neck.

# CHAPTER NINETEEN

## Fish in a Barrel

John caught up to Darrel. Both were out of breath.

"Moose! Argh. Moose, help meeeeee!"

It was Billy. John turned and started to run back for him, but Darrel tackled him to the ground.

"Are you fucking crazy?" Darrel let go of John's legs and stood up. "He's gone!"

John ignored his brother and tried again to go back for Billy. Darrel slid in front of him and pushed him in the chest backwards.

John lost it. He hit Darrel in the face with a right cross. Darrel just took it, and John started pounding him with everything he had. Darrel let him get in a couple of more hits before throwing John to the ground.

"Enough!"

John looked up at him. Darrel was a solid man, a true Moose. John could feel his temper start to rise again. He couldn't understand why Darrel was stopping him. He stood up and started pleading with his brother.

"Billy needs us!"

"It's not Billy, not anymore," Darrel said. "Remember what the old timer told us?"

John gave Darrel a puzzled look. He was trying to remember what the old timer had said.

"About the wind," Darrel said, "how it whispered. How it said his buddy's name."

John remembered the story Sully told in the bar the other night.

"We have to stick together," Darrel said. "If we separate, we're dead. We'll walk back to camp together."

"But what about Karl and Billy? What about Danny? And Sal, he's— "

Darrel grabbed John's shoulders and shook hard. "Dead! They're gone! I need you to focus, little brother!"

John started to calm himself, pushing his anxiety down. John was also aware it could overtake him if he let it. He looked at Darrel and nodded. Darrel looked him in the eyes for a few seconds and then let him go.

"How many bullets do you have?"

John did a quick check of his pockets and rifle. "One in the chamber and five in my pocket."

"I have seven rounds plus this." Darrel raised Sal's cannon and filled it with bullets. Darrel pointed at two balsam firs about thirty feet tall. "I got an idea. Let's climb those trees and see if we can pick a couple off."

John looked at his brother and said, "Those needles are going to suck."

Darrel responded, "I think the needles are the least of our problems."

They walked over to the trees and started climbing them. It did suck. The needles were sharp, and the tree branches were fragile, but they managed to ascend pretty high. The trees were about ten feet apart. Darrel was a few feet higher. He looked down and motioned for John to be quiet.

The surrounding area was full of thickets and an occasional tree, like the ones they were in. The camp was about a mile or so to the east.

They waited for about thirty minutes in their nature-made tree stands. It was still morning, probably around seven or eight. Darrel waved for John's attention and pointed down to where two deer were trotting. They stopped in the spot Darrel and John had been fighting. Blood marred their faces like they had been eating roadkill. That led to dark thoughts John didn't want to entertain. Darrel pointed to one, indicating he was going to shoot. John gave him a thumbs up. They had to coordinate their shots in order to take them both down at the same time.

Darrel whispered, "On three."

We set our sights on our targets.

"One, two, three!"

*Pow! Pow!*

John's doe dropped to the ground, while Darrel's took three steps and then fell. John and Darrel looked at each other. Darrel motioned for quiet and a reload. About five minutes later, another deer showed up. Then, two more emerged from the brush after it. The three walked over and sniffed the bodies of their fallen comrades. Then John was blown away by what happened next. Two of the deer dragged the dead back into the woods. In a few seconds, they were gone. The other doe just stood there, with her tail up. She was nervous. Darrel motioned that he was going to take the shot and lined up his sight.

*Pow!*

Their dad's old 1970 30.30 lever-action Winchester rang true. The doe dropped in her tracks. John looked over at his brother and gave him a thumbs up. Darrel nodded and motioned John to remain silent again, and their sniper game continued.

Four more deer came out a minute later. John couldn't understand it. Every deer he had ever seen or heard of had always run from the sound of a hunting rifle. But not these. They were inquisitive. Unafraid. Two of them walked over and sniffed one of the dead deer. Then, they grabbed it and dragged it back into the bush and disappeared.

Darrel pointed to the other two, and John lined up his target.

*Pow! Pow!*

It was like shooting fish in a barrel. John smiled at Darrel and said, "We're not leaving until we kill every one of these motherfuckers!"

Darrel replied, "I'm not sure we have enough bullets."

A weird howl came from the trees. A roaring animal shriek. A combination of a high pitched scream and a roaring grizzly bear. The same howl they had heard before they found Sal, dead. It sent shivers down John's spine, and Darrel grimaced like he was in pain.

# CHAPTER TWENTY

## "I Say We Go Out Swinging!"

Darrel motioned for silence, and they both reloaded. They waited. Time ticked by. The snow fell softly. The sun rose higher in the sky.

John and Darrel waited for an hour. They were in no hurry to come down from their safe perches. Three dead deer lay untouched below them. The snow started falling thicker, and John shivered in the cold. Darrel was shivering too. In the mayhem this morning, they had run out of the cabin without their jackets.

Darrel whispered to John, "Let's wait a little longer." John nodded, so they waited another thirty minutes. John noticed his breath fogging up the air in front of him as he exhaled.

"I don't think they're coming back."

Darrel looked over at John. They were both frozen solid to the bone. "Well, we either freeze to death up here in these Christmas trees, or we make a run for it."

John looked in his brother's eyes. "I say we go out swinging!"

They climbed down. Needles pricked John's cold skin every step of the way. Then they were on the ground, the three dead deer laid a few feet away.

Darrel looked around. "I think it's safe."

John looked around, too. There was no wind, just the light sound of falling snow.

"I agree," John said. "The camp is less than a mile that way."

Darrel nodded, and they started walking. Quietly, Darrel said, "When we get to the woods, just follow me. I am going to fly, so keep up."

John nodded. The hair on the back of his neck was standing up. Darrel's breath came out in thick clouds. They tried to move fast without making a lot of noise.

Suddenly, a deer appeared about one hundred feet away and made a beeline for us.

"Oh, shit!" Darrel raised his dad's rifle.

*Pow!*

The deer dropped, but two more appeared from the tree line and ran toward the hunters with reckless abandon.

Darrel said, "I got the one on the right."

"Ok."

Darrel ejected the empty shell casing. They both took aim and fired.

*Pow! Pow!*

Both deer went down. John was pumping full of adrenaline; his heart was racing.

"I got two shots left," said Darrel.

Another deer came at them behind Darrel. .

"Kneel!" John said.

Darrel didn't ask why, he knelt. John fired.

*Pow!*

"I have two shots left too." John said.

Darrel looked in every direction. John did the same. They were anticipating another attack. Their eyes were focused on the slightest of movements. John was breathing hard and fast. His sanity was being challenged by his suppressed anxiety.

"Keep it together little brother," Darrel said.

John said nothing, but he appreciated his brother's advice, it helped keep his anxiety at bay.

"How many of these fuckers are there?" Darrel said.

John looked at him and shrugged.

"Three o'clock." he yelled.

Darrel lined up the shot.

*Pow.* It dropped about thirty feet away. "They're all does!" Darrel said. "Other than Billy's buck, they've all been does."

He was right. John wondered where the other bucks were.

"They really want us bad," Darrel said. "It's like they've mutated into zombie deer."

John didn't have time to answer. Three more deer came at them from the trees.

"Johnnie, you're going to have to take the first and last one."

"Ok."

Darrel turned his head and said, "Don't miss."

*Pow! Pow!*

Two fell. The third stopped about fifty feet away from the hunters.

"Take her, Johnnie!"

It snorted and looked right at them. It turned, looking for a moment as if it was going back into the tree line, then it spun around and charged.

*Pow.*

John missed! It wasn't slowing down. When it was almost on top of John, Darrel stepped in front of him and raised Bobby's cannon.

*Boom!*

The deer's face exploded. Blood sprayed all over them. John's ears rang.

Two more deer charged forward. Darrel stepped into the middle of the clearing.

*Boom! Boom!*

They fell at his feet. He turned and looked at John.

"Behind you!"

It was too late. The deer slammed into John's

back and knocked him flat onto his chest. He looked up and saw the deer grinning, but only for a moment.

*Boom!*

The deer fell heavily on top of him. He pushed it off and got to his feet.

Darrel stood in the middle of the killing field. They were still coming, an endless supply of them. John flipped his rifle around and held it like a baseball bat. A deer approached Darrel from his left. John took three steps and swung, chopping the deer down by its legs. It tried to get up, but its legs wouldn't take the weight.

*Boom!*

Another deer went down.

Something hit John hard, and he fell again. His back was on fire, like he'd been stabbed with several knives. He looked up at Darrel. Everything seemed to be in slow motion.

*Boom!*

Darrel ended another deer's life. Another deer approached in the corner of John's vision. He couldn't react in time, and the deer smacked him in the head. He lay on his back staring at the sky. Stars filled his vision.

*Click.*

It was Sal's cannon. Had to be.

*Click! Click!*

John felt himself slipping away like a dream. He thought of Karl and Sal, how funny Billy was, how Danny always laughed at everything. Then everything went black.

# CHAPTER TWENTY-ONE

## "Run Johnnie!"

John woke up when he heard Darrel shouting, "Get the fuck off me!"

John watched in horror as several deer surrounded him, closing in until he couldn't see Darrel anymore.

That terrible howl rent the air again. John froze, every muscle in his body stilled. The deer backed away, revealing Darrel lying on his back. One of them kept him down with its front legs. Darrel turned his head and made eye contact with John. John made an attempt to move toward his brother. Darrel's eyes widened, and he shook his head no. He wanted John to stay still. Something emerged from the tree line. At first, John thought it was Big Charlie, but the beast was bigger than any Adirondack legend he had ever heard of. John counted sixteen points. It had to weigh over three hundred pounds, possibly close to four hundred. This buck probably had eaten Big Charlie. It walked over to Darrel. The other doe took its hooves off Darrel's chest and joined the other deer. They had formed a circle around him a few feet back. The huge buck stood watching Darrel for a long time. Darrel didn't move, he stared back at the beast with contempt. The buck lifted a leg and produced a claw. John thought it looked **like the claw of one of those velociraptors from the Jurassic Park movies**.

Darrel turned to John and mouthed the words "I'm sorry!" Tears ran down John's cheeks. He was powerless to stop what was going to happen next. A sense of self-preservation started creeping in. He thought about escaping. About getting as far away from this place as possible. Then a feeling of guilt hit him. The kind of shame that sets into your soul when you can't save your brother.

Darrel shouted, "Run, Jo—!"

Before Darrell could get the words out of his mouth, the big buck ripped into him with its claw.

John pushed himself up and ran back toward camp. As he reached the edge of the tree line, he stopped and looked back. He wished he hadn't. They were eating Darrel. All of them. The big buck sliced Darrel to pieces while the other deer fed on the strips.

The big man-eating buck lifted its head and seemed to smile at him. Its mouth was full of blood-stained, carnivorous teeth. As if on some signal, two of the deer turned and ran toward him.

John took off. The wind blasted his face. The ground wasn't as alien to him in the daylight. The deer were close behind, but how far? He didn't dare to look. He kept running, leaping and dodging branches. If he could get to camp, he had a chance. He would lock the door and use the wireless to call for help.

"Help meeeeeeee!" The voice came from a thicket to John's left about forty feet away. It sounded like a whisper. It didn't sound like a person begging for help.

He stopped. "Karl, is that you?" Reluctantly, he moved toward the thicket. That guilty feeling hit him again. He couldn't just leave his friends out here, not if there was a chance, he could help them. "Billy, are you there?"

John waited for a reply, but it didn't come. Behind him off in the distance he heard the sounds of deer running in the woods. He started running again. There was really no path, but he found the trail they had made through the brush and followed the boot prints in the snow.  The woods flowed past him on either side.

"Darrel. Help meeeeee!"

He slowed again. This time the voice came from the right. It sounded like... "Danny, is that you?"

Suddenly, something grabbed his foot. John freaked out and screamed, "Argh!" He looked down and saw Billy. His hand grabbed John's boot. John took a closer look and realized Billy was missing fingers. His face was marred by an enormous gash. He was bleeding from his neck, and one of his arms looked broken and gnawed on.

"Oh Billy, I'm so sorry." The tears started running down John's face. His mouth was wide open, he was having trouble comprehending the moment.

"Johnnnnn. Johnnniiieeee. Help me!"

Two deer were in the thicket behind him. They were chewing on Billy's legs. Part of his femur was exposed, the muscle ripped away.

"Make them stoooooop! Please, stoooop!"

John grabbed his hands and pulled. He tried pulling him out.

"Stop!" Billy cried. "It fucking hurts!"

He couldn't just leave him here. John pulled harder in a gruesome tug of war between him and two man-eating deer. Billy was the rope.

"Come on, Billy, we can do this."

John dug his feet in and pulled him harder. Billy's eyes fluttered like he was going to pass out. John got him two feet out of the thicket when he tripped over a stump and landed on his ass. John was still holding onto Billy's hand, but it wasn't attached to Billy anymore. He shuttered and dropped the hand. Before he could grab Billy again, Billy disappeared back into the thicket.

"Johnnieeeeeeee!" His scream faded fast.

By the time John got to his feet, he could barely hear it anymore. Billy was gone. Guilt was creeping in again. He started thinking of Sal, and Darrel. Now he couldn't save Billy.

Suddenly he heard that sound again, the sound deer make when they run through the woods, and it was closer.

He started running again. He passed the fork; the camp wasn't far. The cabin clearing was just up ahead.

The deer were behind him and getting closer. The sound of their hooves trotting in the snow was getting louder. He tried to keep his mind occupied by the wind on his face. The clearing was getting closer now. He could see the chimney stack of the camp through the trees. There was another car parked there. A feeling of hope started flowing through him. More tears fell on his face, he was almost there. A mixture of heavy breathing and joyful crying swept over John. He kept running. A man? Big, wearing a uniform. Yes, it was Phil. John burst out of the woods into the clearing. Phil walked around the cabin toward the front door. He tried to call Phil's name, but he was out of breath. He walked toward the cabin and fell on his face. His back was on fire. He knew this sensation, like the wind on his face when he ran. He started moving backwards, dragged back into the woods.

# CHAPTER TWENTY-TWO

## "That's Just the Wind."

"I don't understand?" Phil said. "I told them about the mountain lion."

George looked at his partner.

"Well, they have gone hunting, regardless. We can leave them a note."

Phil walked back to the car. He noticed movement near the tree line. Something was in the woods. He called to George, and they both walked over to investigate.

Phil looked at his partner. "Did you hear that?"

"Hear what?"

A voice came faintly from the trees. "Help meeeeeeeee!"

"That!" Phil said. "Did you hear it?"

George looked out into the woods, and then back at Phil and said, "That's just the wind."

# Acknowledgements

Gin Matters would like to thank several people, but also include numerous lifetime experiences for helping to collaborate this book. My childhood time spent in the Adirondack mountains helped cement many fond memories and relationships. Swimming in the vast lakes and climbing the great peaks made me appreciate the land they called God's country.

The deer, so many deer. So peaceful and majestic. Their athletic grace helps them negotiate fallen trees, bushes, rocks like they were flying on top of the terrain with ease.

The hunters and their stories of Adirondack folk lore. I must admit, I do enjoy the taste of venison. But I did sometimes root for the deer to win.

The lifelong bonds I created growing up in my youth and the comradery that still endures decades later.

My daughter whom I dubbed, "Hails and bails of hay!" Thank you for believing in me as a writer.

Lastly, I would like to thank my wife. She helped me find the resources and contacts that, facilitated the finishing touches of this story.

# About the Author

**Gin Matters** is an educated man who found his passion for writing later on in life. His creative ideas are from his hot tub spawned adventures. His imagination is greatly influenced by Stephen King, J.R.R. Tolkien, and Gene Roddenberry. Gin strives to be a creative, visual writer that will take you to the edge of your seat and leave you asking for more.

www.ingramcontent.com/pod-product-compliance
Lightning Source LLC
Chambersburg PA
CBHW061220210726
48294CB00006B/1915